<u>THE</u> RAIN MAN

by
James Rada, Jr.

LEGACY
PUBLISHING

A division of AIM PUBLISHING GROUP

OTHER BOOKS BY JAMES RADA, JR.

Beast

Canawlers

Logan's Fire

My Little Angel

To Ben,
who wants to be a policeman...
at least for today.

THE RAIN MAN

Published by Legacy Publishing, a division of AIM Publishing Group.
Cumberland, Maryland.
Copyright © 2002 by James Rada, Jr.
All rights reserved.
Printed in the United States of America.
First printing: June 2002.

ISBN 0-9714599-1-6

Cover photo courtesy of Albert L. Feldstein.

Printed in the United States by Morris Publishing
3212 East Highway 30
Kearney, NE 68847
1-800-650-7888

Library of Congress Control Number: 2002092047

LEGACY
PUBLISHING

P.O. Box 118 • Cumberland, Maryland 21501-0118

HISTORICAL FOREWORD

Our Legacy of Floods
Part 1

By Albert L. Feldstein

It is against a backdrop of natural disaster that the murderous tale of *The Rain Man* unfolds. In this case, the natural disaster is non-fiction, and in my mind, the most-destructive force of its type to ever be inflicted upon the City of Cumberland in Maryland. I speak of the great St. Patrick's Day Flood of March 17, 1936.

We in Allegany County, Maryland, have a continuing historical relationship with the catastrophic forces of nature. Looking through history, it seems every time the snow melted and the rains came, floods deluged this region. Some of the earliest recorded floods go all the way back to 1810 when several bridges in downtown Cumberland were washed out, as well as some extensive flooding in the region now known as Lonaconing.

Lonaconing had a devastating flood in 1884 that wiped out most of the town. This flood actually led to the town incorporating in 1890 so as to provide paved streets and other public improvements. There were other major floods recorded in 1816 and 1828. As a matter of fact, it was during the building of the Chesapeake and Ohio Canal, which reached Cumberland in 1850, that construction suffered major setbacks because of major floods occurring all through the 1830s and 1840s.

With flooding can also come disease. After a major flood in the spring of 1853, the City of Cumberland was covered with mud and other types of filth. As a result, we experienced a cholera epidemic that caused fifty-five deaths and had the town virtually empty of people as everyone headed for the hills after the first confirmed cholera death. The 1850 census indicates that the City of Cumberland had a population of 6,067 people at that time.

1

Popularly known as the "Johnstown Flood," the rainfall and resulting deluge of June 1, 1889, caused great financial and property havoc throughout the Potomac Valley. This mammoth flood heavily damaged the C&O Canal, scattered boats, cost hundreds of jobs and caused enough destruction to close the canal for almost two years to complete the repairs. Although major in its impact, Weather Bureau gauges at the Johnson Street Bridge and the C&O Canal dam indicate 1889 flood marks about four feet below the future 1936 level.

Following the 1889 flood, no other flood of such major proportions would occur over the entire Potomac River Basin until 1924. However, there was some notable flooding in the various tributaries including some serious deluges within the city, primarily occurring in 1894, 1902, 1903, 1905 and 1907. Typical of this would be the flood of February 28, 1902, which, although a tremendous flood with a water flow depth in the Cumberland area of fifteen and a half feet, would still be exceeded by the floods of 1889, 1924 and 1936.

It was the floods of 1924, however, that caused serious damage. In particular, the flood of March 29, 1924, not only left Cumberland, but other areas as well under water. Although the flood of March 29, 1924, was to be definitely exceeded by the 1936 flood in Cumberland, this flood is still characterized by its extraordinary severity along the North Branch of the Potomac River above the city. The towns of Luke and Westernport saw their Potomac River Bridge to Piedmont, West Virginia, washed away.

The West Virginia Pulp and Paper Company and the newly developing Amcelle (American Cellulose and Chemical Manufacturing Company) plant site all suffered physical damage, with the latter suffering further production delays and financial problems with an additional flooding of the Potomac River on May 12, 1924. As a matter of fact, it would not be until Christmas Day of that same year that Amcelle, or Celanese as it became commonly known, would after much effort produce its first cellulose acetate yarn. Just as historically significant, it was also the vast destructive nature of this flood upon the C&O Canal that caused the already financially troubled canal's final termination of operations in 1924.

The melting snow and heavy rains along the streams of the Allegheny Mountain region during March 28 and 29 caused the Potomac River to swell. By 8:30 a.m. on the 29th, Wills Creek overflowed its banks resulting in tremendous havoc and property loss in the Cumberland vicinity. Telephone, telegraph and electric wires were swept away and the city left in darkness. Cumberland's central business district was flooded to a height of four feet. Most of the paving washed away with a torrent of water rushing down Mechanic Street at a great velocity. With the Potomac River rising at a rate of one foot per hour until 3 p.m. and one and a half feet per hour until 6 p.m., half of Cumberland's west side was flooded to a depth of five feet. Property loss, including Western Maryland and Baltimore and Ohio railroad damage and washed-out bridges, was conservatively estimated at between four and five million dollars. The flood of March 29, 1924 had been two and a half feet higher than any previous flood in Cumberland's history. One Potomac River gauge had the river reaching a height of nineteen feet, two and one-half inches. By 5 a.m. on March 30, the water had completely receded and clean-up operations began.

The deluge that soon followed on May 12, 1924, flooded many of the same sections of the city, but not to such a great depth. With water flows about four feet below the earlier March level, losses were approximated at only about $35,000 in Cumberland.

It was then, immediately after the 1924 floods, that people started talking about a flood-control construction project, and a plan was actually developed for the first time. The project called for the construction of flood walls along Wills Creek and deepening the channels and levees along the Potomac River. However, no action was taken on the project at the time. The WPA (Works Progress Administration) crews did some work on the islands of the Potomac in regard to debris removal during the early 1930s, but nothing was actually done to protect the city from the devastation of the St. Patrick's Day Flood of March 17, 1936.

This flood began as a downpour on March 16. By mid-day on St. Patrick's Day, almost three inches of rain had fallen, and it was still coming down. Cumberland's Fire Chief began notifying property owners along Mechanic Street and the low-lying parts of the town to prepare for high water. At this time the water was still nearly eight feet lower than flood stage, but was rising rapidly. The rain, along with the melting snow caused much of Cumberland's central business district (Mechanic, Baltimore, and Liberty Streets) to be under water by mid-afternoon. Many of the first floors of homes and businesses were covered on Mechanic, Baltimore and Greene Streets, and in some areas the water rose to a level well over ten feet.

By 3 p.m., every store owner along the lower end of Baltimore Street had suspended business. Store owners and employees rushed helter-skelter putting merchandise in high places. Among them was my father, who owned Metro Clothes, which at that time was located in the first floor of the old Olympia Hotel that stood on the northwest corner of Baltimore and Mechanic Streets. Unfortunately, the high places proved not high enough in many cases because people thought the water would not rise above the 1924 levels.

Many people who lived or worked on the west side of the city were trapped. We still hear stories of how the B&O Railroad viaduct was the only way to get across town. It began to grow dark. Fear that the electric lights would go out soon grew. Candles became precious and even matches were in great demand. The City Fathers, realizing that Cumberland was in for a siege created flood headquarters at City Hall from which to direct emergency activities. The Red Cross, with its usual dispatch, set up an emergency headquarters at the state armory. Water was two feet deep in the streets by this time and still rising. Every pair of hip boots in town had been sold.

During the flood, a 20,000-gallon gasoline tank was washed into Wills Creek, and it was thought a terrible explosion would occur as it collided with the Valley Street Bridge. WTBO radio warned spectators to avoid the area near the tank because it was going to explode. Naturally, everyone came out onto the bridge to see the explosion. A local postcard sent during this period reads, "We lost everything downstairs in the flood. This is a big gasoline tank which was right across Mechanic Street. If it would of ever bursted or caught fire, how terrible for all. Hope LeRoy, you and Margaret and the boys are well. Marge got her dress. Thanks. Write soon. Love from all, Florence."

Railroad passenger and freight service ceased during the flood. Sixteen people were trapped in a building on South Mechanic Street. Several men were marooned in a cigar store on Centre Street, and later nearly drowned when the water broke a glass plate window and swept them out into the stream. Nearly every store on Baltimore Street held refugees.

As night wore on, rescue crews provided food to the buildings by pulleys, but evacuating the victims was impossible. All banks, movie theaters and businesses were closed, and the National Guard was called out to keep order. Trains, buses and cars were stranded. Communications were cut off, and the city was isolated for the duration of the high water, save for WTBO, which obtained permission to stay on the air all night. Hotels outside the flooded area were packed, and hundreds spent the night in the state armory cared for by the Red Cross, which estimated the number of families washed out of their homes at 1,200, close to 6,000 people. A Mechanic Street resident wrote at the time, "We live just up the street a space on Mechanic. I never seen so much water and refuse come down the street like a ocean. I prayed all night long so our house would still be here in the morning."

The George's Creek communities, including Midland, Lonaconing, Barton and Westernport, which was reported to have water waist deep, also suffered heavily from the floods. The waters not only damaged the railroad lines, streets and sewers, but also inundated area mines. This calamity was the final straw for several of the local coal enterprises that were already in financial trouble. In Lonaconing, Mayor William O. Jones estimated the damage to be $50,000.

But it was in Cumberland that the hardship and devastation was so bad, that the Mayor and City Council went so far as to publish a notice, in the public interest of course, that the selling of intoxicating liquors in the city, including wines and beers, would be illegal until the flood emergency passed. Most movie theaters, including the Strand, Embassy, Liberty, and Garden were closed as a result of the damage. However, the Maryland Theater, because of its high concrete and stone entrance on Mechanic Street, suffered only slightly. It reopened on March 21, with a Laurel and Hardy film entitled, "Bohemian Girl". No sooner had the flood started to subside, than work began on the repair of water lines. Whole companies of Civilian Conservation Corps workers were rushed in. The city hired scores of workers, and private contractors along with their men and equipment were pressed into service. The damaged areas were sealed off, and no one allowed to enter except on business. Reconstruction work progressed rapidly. Plate glass poured into the town and over 300 boarded-up windows were replaced the day after the flood. The National Guard was recalled, as were the State Police and Special Officers, and the Great Flood of 1936 became history.

The St. Patrick's Day Flood of March 17, 1936, got the flood-protection initiative going, and in 1936, the United States Senate approved the first of several appropriations for a flood-control construction project to include not only the North Branch of the Potomac River, but also Wills Creek. Levees, retaining walls, channel clearing and deepening were all included. As a matter of fact, the Army Corps of Engineers had actually developed definite design plans by 1940. On April 25, 1936, the United States Senate Commerce Committee had reported a bill that appropriated $900,000 for flood-control protection for Cumberland, Maryland, and Ridgeley, West Virginia. This bill became the Flood Control Act of 1936. A new Flood Act in 1938, and another in 1946, supplemented the original 1936 legislation. The administration of President Franklin Delano Roosevelt, our United States Senators from both Maryland and West Virginia, and our local Maryland Congressman David J. Lewis, all played critical roles in establishing the authority and groundwork for the eventual construction of the Flood Control Project. However, a little something called World War II came up, and everything was shelved for the duration.

There were many people who played a role in providing local flood relief after the 1936 flood. These included Maryland Governor Harry W. Nice who visited the flood sites and took steps to provide relief and funds. Our Congressional representatives, led by Congressman David J. Lewis, began to press for flood-control protection funds from the federal government. State Senator Robert B. Kimble of Allegany County sought flood-relief funds from the State. Allegany County Commissioners A. Charles Stewart, James Holmes and Nelson W. Russler floated local bond bills for flood assistance. Cumberland Mayor George W. Legge and Mayor-Elect Thomas W. Koon, M.D. worked together to raise funds and begin work with the Army Corps of Engineers to develop a long-term solution to flooding in Cumberland and the entire Potomac River Valley. The Allegany County Flood Disaster Committee included Mrs. George Henderson of the Allegany County Red Cross, Dr. Joseph Franklin as the Allegany County Health Officer, Lt. Col. George Henderson representing the Maryland National Guard, Harry Greenstein from the Maryland Emergency Relief Administration and J. Milton Patterson of the Allegany County Welfare Board.

I hope you enjoy reading *The Rain Man*. To me, aside from being a swell murder mystery, the real fascination comes from Jim Rada's weaving of actual historical events, Cumberland locations, and even real persons into the telling of this story. Look for these.

December 28, 2001

6

The Rain Man

Al Feldstein is an award-winning local historian. He has published twenty-six books, prints, posters and videotapes depicting the history of all three Western Maryland counties — Allegany, Garrett and Washington. For his work in the preservation and promotion of the history and culture of Western Maryland, Feldstein received a National Commendation in 1991 from the American Association for State and Local History, and in 1993, was honored by the Maryland Historical Trust with their Preservation Service Award. For his efforts in developing and promoting the regional hospitality industry, he was presented the 1995 Allegany County Tourism Award. He received a Governor's Citation in 1997 for his Civic Leadership and Efforts in the Promotion of Western Maryland History and Culture.

1

Monday, March 16, 1936
7:03 p.m.

Raymond Twigg raised his hands into the dark evening sky as if praying to an ancient god. In response, the skies opened up and rain began to fall lightly, but steadily, on his palms and face. Raymond allowed the cold water to rinse the fresh blood from his hands. The raindrops fell softer than the flow from his apartment shower. The rain caressed him, thanking Raymond for his offering.

The raindrops lifted the blood from his hand and mixed with it. The red raindrops ran together growing larger and larger. They ran down his arms in small, red rivers until it appeared Raymond was wearing a shirt with red-striped sleeves.

"Be free from sin, my son," he said to himself. Then he laughed loudly into the dark sky. His laugh was a phlegm-filled gurgle that brought no smile to his lips.

His hands clean, Raymond splashed water on his face. He tilted his head back and let the rain fill his mouth. Then he swallowed.

"God's tears at what I've done, but God is no match for the Rain Man," Raymond whispered.

God always cried when the Rain Man took over.

Raymond turned slowly in a circle and held his arms straight out.

When he lowered his head, he saw the body lying at his feet. The dead man's knees were pulled up to his chest so that he lay in a fetal position. The man had tried to protect himself, but there was no protection from the Rain Man.

"Beware the ides of March," Raymond said and laughed again. The laugh changed gradually, growing higher in pitch and less strained. Then it cut off abruptly.

Raymond circled the body, staring down at it as if it were the first time he had seen the man. The dead man was dressed in overalls. He might have been a farmer who had come into Cumberland for a drink or two after buying seed and supplies for the coming season. He might have been a railroader who had finished work at the B&O rail yard and was headed home for the night.

He might have been anyone because Raymond didn't know him.

Raymond nudged the body with the toe of his boot. The body rolled onto its back. Rain fell into the man's wide-open eyes. The side of his head was bloody and oddly dented from where Raymond had hammered the man's head against the brick alley until the sound of breaking bone had told him the man was dead.

"You shouldn't have done it," Raymond said, shaking his head.

He squatted beside the man and stretched the body out on its back. The least he could do was to let people think this man had died like a man should and not curled up in a ball, crying like a baby.

Done what? the Rain Man's voice asked in Raymond's head.

"Killed him. You killed this man."

Raymond crossed the man's arms over his chest just like the funeral directors did with the dead bodies that they handled. This man didn't smell of formaldehyde and make-up. How could he be dead?

I didn't kill him. I freed you from the pain. Isn't that what you always ask for? To be free from the pain? This is the way, the Rain Man said in a mocking tone.

"I don't want to be free this way," Raymond said.

It is the only way you will be free from the pain.

The Rain Man never felt Raymond's pain. He didn't care about Raymond's pain. He caused pain; he didn't end it. The Rain Man thought Raymond was just a cry baby. That just proved to Raymond that the Rain Man didn't know everything. He didn't know how to make the pain stop for good. Or, if he did, he would not tell because he didn't want to release Raymond from his control.

"I'm the one in pain. Why don't you free me from my pain? Why does it always have to come back?" Raymond asked.

Oh? You want to be like him? That's the only way to stop the pain.

"Then you admit you killed him. You admit he's dead." When Raymond didn't feel the pain, he could think clearly and argue better with the Rain Man. Not that it ever did him any good.

I didn't kill him. You did. The blood was on your hands. Those same hands slammed him against the bricks in the street until his skull cracked like an eggshell.

Raymond looked at his hands. He held them up before his face. He watched the rain hit his fingers and run down the sides of his knuckles to mix with blood that still remained in the flesh between his fingers. The Rain Man was right. The dead man's blood was on his hands. The death was on his conscience just like the other ones.

Raymond let his hands fall to his sides. He always broke first. He always listened to the Rain Man and not the other way around.

The pain was gone for now, but Raymond had another worry.

"What have you done?" Raymond whispered.

I helped you make the pain go away, the Rain Man bragged.

"But you made me kill someone again."

No, I made the pain go away. You killed that man.

Raymond shook his head and sobbed. He didn't understand how this happened or how to make it stop.

"But the pain will return. It always does. This man won't live again," Raymond said.

Perhaps. Perhaps not. I still live.

"To torment me."

To offer salvation. To offer justice. To offer peace. To offer...

"Death."

The Rain Man laughed. *That is what I said. Death is salvation. Death is the ultimate justice. It is your peace.*

Raymond could feel the pain beginning to build again. It started in one spot, generally at the back of his head. It began as a dull throbbing. Then the throbbing would spread and Raymond would feel as if his head was in a vise. The pressure seemed to be everywhere at once. The pain was sometimes so bad that he passed out, but he hadn't passed out this time. The body at his feet told him that.

This time, the pain was going to be bad. He had thought it couldn't get as bad as it had this afternoon, but it was already returning. The pain always went away when he killed it. For it to return so soon was a bad sign. It meant the Rain Man would want something more in exchange for stopping Raymond's pain.

Raymond pulled his attention away from the body and looked around himself. He had to get away from here before someone found the body with him standing over it. No one would believe it was the Rain Man who had killed this man and not Raymond.

It wasn't me. It was you, said the Rain Man.

Raymond wiped his face, flicking away the rain running down his bulbous nose and square chin. He felt as if he was crying...he should be crying. Was he wiping away his tears along with the rain?

He was in a dark alley. Either morning hadn't arrived or the rain was holding it at bay. Raymond couldn't make out any details to know in which alley he was standing. He remembered going into a bar on Virginia Avenue after he had finished greeting mourners at the funeral home where he worked. He had left his job early because of the pain pounding in his head. That had been about six o'clock. Was it still the same night? Was he still in South Cumberland?

Raymond preferred Johnny's Place, but he also frequently visited the other bars in the area. Since Prohibition had ended three years ago, liquor flowed freely in Allegany County, and Raymond had developed an appreciation for alcohol's medicinal qualities. Sometimes liquor helped stop the pain or at least make it not hurt as much. Raymond much preferred whiskey to the Rain Man.

Raymond walked slowly to the end of the alley, ready to dive into the shadows should someone happen along. He couldn't let himself be caught with a dead man and blood on his clothes. He rested his back against the corner of a building and took a deep breath. If someone recognized him coming out of the alley, they might be able to identify him for the police.

Raymond stepped out into the street and continued walking. He nearly ran at first until he was a dozen yards away. Then he slowed to a normal walk and caught his breath. It took him two blocks before he recognized where he was. This was North Centre Street. He was on the opposite side of town from where he remembered being last night. Sometime between when he went into Johnny's Place and when he stepped out onto North Centre Street, he had killed a man.

He glanced at the brick homes around him, looking for a peering face behind a curtained window. No one stared back. The street was empty since it was still early and dreary out. No cars were on the road. Most porch lights were dark, and the dark sky would help hide him. Raymond had been lucky. It seemed that no one had seen him.

If only the rain would stop. The pain was always worse when it was raining and the Rain Man was always angrier and stronger.

Raymond's stomach rumbled and he wondered how long it had been since he had eaten. He remembered wanting to eat dinner after work, but he couldn't remember if he had actually eaten. Maybe, he'd go home and eat and hope that the pain wouldn't get worse.

If it did, he didn't know what the Rain Man would do.

2

Monday, March 16, 1936
7:12 p.m.

Jake Fairgrieve stepped from the protection of the porch down the three steps into the steady evening rain. He shook his head and then tucked his chin in close enough to touch his chest to try and keep at least some of the water out of his face. Not only was the rain pounding him from above, but the large raindrops would strike the wet ground, splashing water upward. It would have gone up over the edge of his shoes if he hadn't been wearing black, rubber overshoes.

It was cold rain. He would have expected it to be warm since the air was, but it felt like tiny pieces of ice hitting him. Jake pitied anyone on foot patrol today, which would be just about all the cops on the force. The Cumberland Police Department had forty officers but only eight pieces of motorized equipment and two of those were motorcycles. He and the rest of the police force would be drenched before the end of the day. They probably wouldn't dry out until next week and probably wouldn't thaw out until next month.

Jake pulled his cap down tighter on his head and snapped his yellow rain slicker closed to the neck. He didn't use an umbrella. Holding one hindered his hands, but more so, police officers just didn't use them. They needed to keep their hands free.

He walked east on Fayette Street from where his two-story house was located on a lot that sat in the shadow of the Washington Street hill. Jake crossed the brick street and went through the gate of Rose Hill Cemetery. He followed the road upward around the hill to where he could see the new Allegany High School beyond the cemetery grounds. Sometimes he imagined that Rose Hill was not actually a hill at all but a pile of bodies that had simply had a layer a top soil thrown over them. In a way, he guessed it was.

Jake left the cemetery road and crossed the soggy ground. The ground squished under the weight of his steps and threatened to suck his feet into the mud. It was a familiar walk. He could have closed his eyes and still walked here. In fact, he had climbed the iron fence on a few moonless nights when he couldn't sleep and made his way here in the dark.

He stopped by instinct more than seeing the grave site in the dark.

The headstone at his feet was a simple, rectangular piece of granite. His

The Rain Man

friends and family had offered to loan him money for a better memorial, but Jake had thanked them and refused their offers. He had raided his savings to pay for the small granite slab.

He let his fingers trace the engraved letters in the granite. The rain ran down the face of the stone like tears being shed from unseen eyes.

MELISSA ANN FAIRGRIEVE
FEBRUARY 18, 1901 — MARCH 29, 1924
"A LOVE THAT WILL NOT END."

He had chosen this spot especially for his wife. Melissa's grave was high enough up the hill so that it would never see flooding. She would never again be under water even if she had to be underground. It was a difference he appreciated even if Mel couldn't.

"I thought that all of the rain might be scaring you, Mel," Jake said. He knew his wife was dead, but he hoped that somewhere, if Heaven truly existed, she could hear him. "I know I sure get scared every time it rains in March. I'd stay home if I didn't have to work. The chief wouldn't think much of me if he knew I was afraid of the rain." Actually, it wasn't the rain that Jake feared, but what it could do.

Jake took a deep breath and closed his eyes. He listened to the rain beat on his hat and imagined how it would feel to not know it was rain that was hitting you.

When he opened his eyes, he stared at a small vase of yellow and red flowers that he could barely see in the dark. As he watched, raindrops hammered the petals. They wavered under the onslaught. Then a yellow petal fell to the ground, followed shortly thereafter by another yellow petal.

Jake said, "I see your mother brought some more flowers for you, but the rain is beating them silly. I'll have to go see your parents sometime. I know I always say that, but I do mean it. Truly I do."

The last time he had seen his former mother-in-law, Ruth Pittman had been placing flowers on Melissa's grave. Mel had always loved flowers. Her gardens in the backyard of their home were overgrown with weeds because Jake hadn't tended them after she had died. He and Ruth had talked for a short time about missing Mel and how he was doing. Ruth had kissed him on the cheek and Jake had promised to stop by and visit. He hadn't. That had been over a year ago.

"I talked Christine into going camping with me. She and I have some things to work out between us. I've told you about the problems I have with her, and I'm sure you have an endless list of problems she could have with me. I wonder if we can resolve them. Sometimes I wonder if I'm pushing her because I know she won't let our relationship go beyond a certain point and I don't want to be the one to break it off. Stupid, huh? I'm sure I'll make more mistakes, and probably bigger ones, before I finally die."

Jake shifted uneasily from foot to foot as if waiting for a response but heard nothing but the steady thrum of the rain.

"Sometimes, I'm lonely, Mel. I'm so lonely that I cry. Then I think about what not being lonely means I would have to do and that hurts just as much." He watched the rain mix with the dirt on the ground and make mud. "I don't want to put you to the back of my mind. I don't want to move on with my life. I want you. I want to be with you."

He stood there not knowing what more to say. Finally, he sighed and said, "I'm getting drenched standing here, Mel. I'd better go, but I'll be back. I always do."

Jake turned away and trudged slowly back to the road, careful not to slip and fall in the wet grass.

He always felt the need and the duty to visit Melissa's grave, but he rarely felt good upon leaving. How could he, knowing that he was the reason his wife had died? He had failed the most-important person in his life when she had needed him the most. Besides, Jake always felt worse in March. And when it rained in March, he was nervous and always expecting the worse.

He walked from Fayette Street going up the hill on Allegany Street to Washington Street and then headed into town past the large homes of Cumberland's affluent. The homes were owned by businessmen, doctors and politicians and were a mix of architectural styles, such as Queen Anne, Colonial Revival and Greek Revival.

Past the elegant homes, he walked by the county courthouse on Prospect Square and Emmanuel Episcopal Church on the hill leading down to Wills Creek. The church was a Cumberland landmark because it sat on the hill that overlooked Baltimore Street in Downtown Cumberland, but it also sat on the grounds of the old Fort Cumberland, the old frontier fort that gave Cumberland, Maryland, its name.

Jake paused on the Baltimore Street Bridge over Wills Creek and looked at the water. The water level was about eight feet below the bridge. The water was running fast from the north, but it didn't seem to be rising. He looked further south to where the creek fed into the Potomac River. The river didn't look noticeably high either.

So far, so good.

Jake could still remember the first flood of 1924 on March 29. No matter how much he wanted to forget it, he would never be able to do it. The rising Potomac River had put Cumberland under five feet of water. It had been the worst flood the city had seen since 1889 and wasn't something Jake wanted to see again. He hated the water, mainly because he didn't know how to swim.

He finished crossing the bridge and walked down Baltimore Street to Henny's Home-Cooking Restaurant. It was past the Embassy Theater and across the street from Cumberland Cloak and Suit. Traffic was beginning to slow down as people got home from work or the rain drove shoppers inside. He stepped inside the small restaurant and shook the water off his rain slicker.

A counter ran along one side of the restaurant. The grill was behind the counter along with cabinets and refrigerators that held the food items. The counter had eight stools in front of it. There were also three booths and four tables for larger groups. Framed pictures of Art Henny, the owner and cook of the luncheonette, and his wife and six kids over the years hung on the walls.

Jake had never seen the restaurant more than a quarter full and that was before the depression started. He wondered, or rather, he suspected, how Art had kept the luncheonette running. More than one restaurant had fronted for a speakeasy during Prohibition. Of course, Jake hadn't looked too hard for liquor in Art's place and Art hadn't given himself away.

"I keep the door closed because I don't want rain inside and here you come and bring a gallon of it in with you," said Art.

He stood behind the counter watching Jake. Art was a huge man, both in height and width. He wore grease-spattered pants and a shirt, which had undoubtedly started out this morning as crisp white work clothes.

"Talk to God, not to me. I didn't send the rain," Jake replied.

Jake took off his hat and slicker and hung them on the coat hook where the water dripping off them began to form a puddle on the tiled floor. He had to admit that it was quite a bit of water.

"Well God's not here so I'll give you the mop and let you take care of the mess," Art said.

Jake ran his hand through his blond hair and walked over to the counter and sat down. It was still dry…at least for the time being.

"I'll leave you a big tip to cover it," Jake said.

"Don't worry about him, Jake. His knee's acting up again," Harvey McIntyre told him.

Harvey was one of the regulars at Henny's just like Jake. Harvey was a few years older than Jake. He claimed to be a prize fighter who had fought in the 1920s, but he worked at the Celanese Plant now. Of course, Harvey's nose had been busted a few times and his right ear looked perpetually swollen so there might have been something to his story.

Jake came to Henny's for a meal more days than not. For thirty cents, he could get a filling breakfast or dinner (depending on which shift he was working) that would carry him through until he scratched up something at his house for supper or breakfast. Sometimes one of his relatives would stop in to check up on him and bring a meal. He appreciated the meals and his family's concern, but he still could have done without the prying small talk to see if he was all right, if he was eating, if he was doing his laundry and whom he was dating. Jake tried to tell his family that he was fine, but they still kept coming.

"You can joke all you want, but I told you yesterday it was going to rain because of the way my knee was feeling," Art said defensively.

"Hell, Art, all anyone had to do was look at the sky and know rain was on its way. It didn't take a psychic knee to make that prediction," Bill Collier said. He was another regular. He worked at Footer's Dye Works just a couple blocks away on South Mechanic Street. He was half a dozen years younger than Jake and had a wife and three kids. He had the life Jake had imagined he would have, but Jake had lost his chance twelve years ago.

"I'm not saying I knew it was just going to rain. I know it's going to be a gully washer of a storm," Art corrected him.

"Good," Bill said, waving an arm toward Baltimore Street. "Maybe it will rain hard enough to wash off the city. The soot is starting to build up again."

Jake and Harvey laughed. It was hard for Cumberland to look clean with all the trains moving through the city each day, puffing smoke and soot out of the smokestacks. Art just scowled at Bill.

Waving a finger under Bill's nose, Art said, "You mark my words or at least my knee. You're not going to be laughing when this rain is done. My knee hurts so bad that I can barely stand this morning let alone walk."

Bill held up his hands in surrender. "I'm not laughing now. I don't like being wet. I'd rather your knee tell me when it's going to be a sunny day."

"Why don't you use an umbrella?" Harvey asked Jake, starting a new line of conversation.

"And how many police officers do you see using umbrellas?" Jake replied.

"All the ones who work outside in the rain and don't have pneumonia," Harvey snapped as he smiled.

Jake and the others in the luncheonette chuckled.

"I'll take my chances. As long as it's not flooding, I won't complain," Jake said. The way Jake saw it, if he went to the trouble of staying away from water any deeper than the depth he filled his bathtub to, then the least the water could do was to stay away from him.

Art slid a plate in front of Jake. It had a thick slice of ham with a pineapple ring on top of it, a piece of buttered toast and a small salad on it. Then Art set a glass of Coca-Cola down next to it.

"What would you do if I ordered something different?" Jake asked, looking from the plate to Art.

"I would think you were sick," Art grumbled.

He stood staring at Jake with his arms crossed over his chest. His dark eyes narrowed and he scowled.

"I'm not sick. I was just wondering that's all," Jake said defensively.

Jake cut a piece off of the ham and ate it. Not all of the regulars came here to eat. Eating out was a luxury that many people couldn't afford in 1936. Jake was single and had a good job, though. He didn't mind giving Art some business, especially when it saved him the trouble of cooking. It meant that he could sleep later before heading to work. Besides, he liked to come into the restaurant to eat and talk to other people. His house could get very lonely at night with no one to talk to. Of course, he'd never tell his family that. Jake had enough siblings, cousins, aunts and uncles so that one of them could stop by every day for two months and Jake wouldn't see the same face twice.

"So what's in the news?" Bill asked.

Jake shrugged. He hadn't read the evening paper.

"It's looks like Bruno Hauptman is still going to die at the end of the month. Governor Hoffman is backing off his support for Hauptman," Art told them.

Bruno Hauptman had been convicted of kidnapping and murdering Charles Lindbergh's son. New Jersey's Governor Hoffman had tried to argue that Hauptman wasn't the only guilty party and attempted to delay the execution. It hadn't worked, though, and Hauptman was still scheduled to die at the end of the month.

"The city election's tomorrow, too," Harvey said. "So are you going to be watching to polls tomorrow?" He directed the last comment to Jake.

Mayor George Legge was running against Thomas Koon in tomorrow's election. Eight other people were running to fill the four city council seats. Watching the polls was not how Jake wanted to spend St. Patrick's Day, but he was working tomorrow night. He would most likely be assigned to a polling place for the city election.

Jake nodded between bites. When he swallowed he said, "I suppose I'll pull a few hours duty in the evening before they close to make sure there's no problem."

"Do you think Legge will win re-election?"

Jake shrugged. "It's hard to say. Koon has plenty of support."

Bill drained the rest of his apple juice and stood up to stretch. "I hate Mondays."

"You hate to work is what you hate," Art commented.

Bill worked down the street at Footer's Dye Works as a cleaner. Footer's was known internationally for their quality cleaning work, but Bill had hinted from time to time that the work load was not what it had been when he started there in 1921. Footer's had cleaned the rugs and linens of the White House and now it was being brought down by local dry-cleaning businesses, which offered decent quality at a much lower cost than Footer's.

Art wiped his hands on his apron and walked over to stare out the window at the falling rain. He shook his head and then flipped a lock of loose, gray hair back into place.

"Do you think it will flood?" he said to no one in particular.

"It's only been raining for an hour," Jake said quickly.

"But my knee tells me…"

Jake cut him off. "The Potomac's not that high. I looked coming across the bridge. Start worrying when the snows melt off the mountains. They measured it forty inches deep this season. That will turn into a lot of water come spring. If it's raining when those snows melt, we'll have problems."

Harvey snorted. "I thought that you had to be observant to be a cop, Jake. Those snows are already melting and this rain will just help it along."

"Well, the river's not high."

"Yet," Harvey corrected him.

Art said, "Nothing will beat 1924. You could have gone swimming in here then."

Jake shuddered and then hoped that no one had seen him.

"Why are we talking about floods when it's just a shower? It probably won't last the night," Jake said.

Bill shrugged and said, "Cumberland's due."

Cumberland's last big flood had been in 1924. The March flood had done four million dollars worth of damage to Cumberland. Jake remembered the flood waters had been a fast-moving river through the city. He had nearly died in the flood and his wife had been killed. It wasn't a time that Jake liked to recall or think about happening again.

"You guys won't see me next week," Jake said, changing the subject.

"Why not? Did you finally realize that Art can't cook?" Bill asked. Art threw a dish towel at the man. Bill ducked and it went flying over him.

Jake shook his head.

"No, I'm going on vacation. I'm going to ride my motorcycle up to Swallow Falls and do some camping for a few days," Jake told them.

"Then you will probably be missing Art's cooking if you're going to have to eat all your own food for a week," Harvey said.

Jake was looking forward to getting away from the city. It had been a year since he had taken any time off work. He hadn't felt comfortable going on vacation when others were scraping by to make ends meet. Still, Jake decided it was time that he and Christine hashed things out between them. Either they were going to get married or they were going to go their separate ways. No more of her "I love you, but..." Jake was also going to have to overcome his own challenges. He wondered if a week would be long enough. He hoped so.

Then again, maybe he didn't hope so.

He just didn't know.

Jake was thirty-six years old. He was a widower who still had a lot of years ahead of him, and he was in love with Christine Evans who was easily the most-pig-headed woman in Allegany County. That's what made them a perfect match. Jake was probably the most-pig-headed man in Allegany County.

Jake sipped his Coca-Cola and turned to look at the rain coming down outside. He sure hoped it didn't rain like this when he and Christine were at the falls. He didn't want the rain to serve as a constant reminder of his past while he was trying to forge his future.

The rain had to stop soon. It had to.

3

Monday, March 16, 1936
7:38 p.m.

Chris Evans ignored the stares from passersby as she walked up the cement stairs and into Memorial Hospital. Knowing she was shocking people out of their complacency, Chris actually enjoyed the attention and would have stared back at the people staring at her if she'd been in a good mood. It wasn't because she was an attractive redhead that earned her the looks of people moving in and out of the hospital. She was wearing pants. Although Memorial wasn't as conservative as Allegany Hospital on Decatur Street, Chris was liberal enough to make even Memorial's doctors seem like priests.

"Good morning, Dr. Evans," the receptionist in the admitting room said.

Chris just nodded. She liked the sound of her title because so few people would have associated it with her. She was a doctor and she was a woman. What's more, she was better than some of the male doctors, which galled them to no end.

Chris was glad for Memorial Hospital because even with all the troubles she had working here, she knew she would never have been able to work at Allegany Hospital with the Daughters of Charity always complaining about her not knowing her place. Didn't they realize that Chris was doing for women what their hospital did for the sick? She was helping to heal their ills and show them that women could be leaders.

Memorial Hospital had been in South Cumberland since 1929. Chris had been here since 1934. She realized how lucky she had been to get the job, because even at her bargain rate, the hospital still hadn't wanted to take Chris on.

After she had graduated from medical school, she had sent her credentials to the superintendent of Memorial. She had used the name Chris Evans rather than Christine Evans because she didn't want the fact that she was a woman to immediately exclude her from consideration of a position with the hospital. Her grades were good enough to get her an interview at the hospital. Of course, the superintendent had nearly fallen out of his chair when Chris walked into his office and introduced herself.

He had reluctantly hired her. It wasn't that William Finn couldn't work

19

with a woman — the assistant superintendent, Katherine Obert, was a woman — he just hadn't liked what he considered deception on Chris's part. Chris hadn't liked it, either, and she had been trying to make it up to him since then by working harder than anyone else on staff worked.

She walked down the hallway until she came to the doctors' lounge. It was late and no one was inside the room. She took the list of her patients from inside her mail cubbyhole and scanned it to see how many patients she wanted to look in on before she headed home.

Chris kept her hair bobbed short, which kept it out of her face when she worked. She put on a white coat and put her list of patients on a clipboard.

What had put her in a bad mood this evening was actually a who...Jake Fairgrieve.

How could she have allowed herself to be talked into going camping next week with the man? She knew she was hard-headed, but she didn't think she held a candle to Jake. The man hadn't been willing to take no for an answer. The more Chris resisted, the more he pressed, but never in a disagreeable way. He had overwhelmed her with kindness to the point that she had felt it would have been downright rude for her to say no. Chris had finally gotten so tired of telling him no without giving him a reason that she had agreed to go with him on his vacation if only he would leave and let her work.

Now if she backed out of the trip, he would think it was because she was afraid to be alone in the woods with a man.

Well, she wasn't. She wasn't afraid of Jake or any man.

If Jake thought camping would put her at a disadvantage, he was sadly mistaken. Besides, it was time they set things straight between the two of them. Jake thought he was going to tie her down to a home and children while he went off and walked the streets of Cumberland in uniform, but she intended to disabuse him of that notion next week.

Jake was a wonderful man, but he was still a man. He still had his chauvinistic ideas of the roles of a man and a wife. He would never be able to accept her as his wife, at least not the type of wife that Chris intended to be.

She didn't really think he wanted to get married, anyway. Jake was still in love with his dead wife.

Chris walked out into the hallway and headed for the first room on her list. As she passed an open door, a patient called out. "Nurse, nurse."

Chris was tempted to ignore the man, but this was just part of the job that she had to do. Besides, the patient obviously needed to be set straight about a few things.

She stopped and frowned at the man. He was lying in his bed with his legs in casts.

"Nurse, can you get me a glass of water? I'm thirsty as the dickens," the man said. He was middle-aged with a bushy beard.

"I'm not a nurse," Chris told him.

The Rain Man

"I'm sorry, ma'am. You're wearing white so I thought that you worked here."

"I do. I'm a doctor."

"A doctor." The man chuckled. "A doctor? That's pretty funny. Can you get me a drink, nurse? My throat feels like sandpaper."

Chris arched an eyebrow. "My name is not Nurse. It's Dr. Evans. I'll tell a nurse what you want," she said firmly.

The man drew back a bit at her tone. "Thank you."

Chris turned to leave and the man asked, "You're not really a doctor, are you?"

She stopped and said, "Yes, I'm really a doctor."

Then the man shook his head and frowned. "Well, now I know the world's going to hell in a handbasket."

Chris stomped down the hallway before she said something she would regret. She was used to people's ignorance about her position. She could even tolerate the hostility if it wasn't for one thing. It wasn't just the men who resisted accepting her as a doctor. The women in this town were just as bad!

Didn't they realize their own stereotypes of themselves were as much responsible for holding them down as the men in this county?

Chris had to give Jake that much credit. At least he didn't pretend to humor her as if she was playing at being a doctor. She *knew* she was a good doctor!

She had met him when he had brought a stabbing victim into the hospital one Friday night last summer. There'd been a fight at a bar on Wineow Street and one man had stabbed another over a spilled drink. Jake had dressed the victim's wound and rushed him to the hospital while another officer arrested the man with the knife.

Jake had carried the man in and laid him on the floor. Then he'd gotten out of the way when he saw Chris. He hadn't even asked her if she could get a doctor to help the man. He had simply backed away and done whatever she asked in order to help the man.

The only surprise he had registered at finding out that she was a doctor was a slight widening of the eyes. If he had had any sharp comments, he had wisely kept them to himself.

She loved it when a man knew when to keep his mouth shut.

And she loved Jake. She just didn't think that he truly loved her.

As she left the room and continued down the hall, she saw Vincent Rutherford, the medical examiner, walking in her direction. Chris groaned and considered changing direction, but that would just be showing him that she was afraid of him. It would be showing weakness, which she refused to do.

He stopped in front of her and smiled.

"Good morning, Chris." He refused to acknowledge that she was a doctor.

"Dr. Rutherford," she replied.

"Don't be like that, Chris." His tone dripped with condescension.

Chris sighed. "I have work to do, doctor."

"You work too hard, Chris. Why don't you come downstairs with me, and I can show you a good time?" Rutherford offered.

She could imagine what he considered a good time. She had heard some of the nurses speaking about visits to the morgue in the basement and the sofa in Rutherford's office.

"The nurses might be impressed with your good times, but I'm not," Chris told him.

He glanced behind himself, then behind her. He turned the knob on the supply room door near them and pushed it open.

"Then I guess we don't have to go downstairs," Rutherford said.

He put an arm around Chris and pushed her into the supply room with a quick shove. Once inside, he shut the door behind them and blocked Chris from it.

"What are you doing?" Chris demanded.

"I thought that you might want to be alone."

More likely, he didn't want to be seen, Chris reasoned.

"I don't have time for this childishness, doctor. I have work to do," Chris insisted.

"Is this childishness?" he asked as he leaned over and tried to kiss her.

Chris pushed him away. He grabbed her by the shoulders and pulled her closer.

In a panic, Chris kneed him in the groin. Rutherford gasped and let her go. He dropped to his knees, holding his groin and trying to catch his breath.

Chris grabbed him by his lab coat and pulled him away from the door. Then she opened the door.

As she started to leave, Rutherford said, "You'll come around, Chris, and when you do, I'll make sure you feel just as much pleasure as pain."

He grinned, which amazed her given his condition, but she didn't think on it too long. She quickly left the supply room.

Chris hurried down the hallway to the first room on her list. She stopped outside the door, took a deep breath and then forced a smile onto her face. She didn't feel cheerful, but if she could make her patients feel happy, she knew it would help their recoveries.

Besides, the last thing she needed was complaints to the hospital superintendent about her being a bitch doctor.

But should she report Rutherford to Dr. Finn, the hospital superintendent?

Chris shook her head. Finn would just think she was weak. He would feel his worries about having her on staff were justified.

She reached out to open the door to the patient's room and noticed her hand was shaking. She drew it back and held it with her other hand to stop the tremors. She took a deep breath and reached out again. Her hand shook.

The Rain Man

Chris turned away from the room and hurried back to the doctors' lounge. Inside the empty room, she took a deep breath and tried to calm her racing heart. Chris walked across the room into the bathroom and locked herself inside. Then she sat on the toilet, buried her face in her hands and cried as softly as she could.

Once started, her sobs were hard to control, though. She cried in great, heaving gasps that left her wanting breath. Tears rolled down her cheeks and pooled in her hands.

Why couldn't these men just accept that she was a doctor and let her do her job? Finn and Rutherford were the worst. Finn was always trying to find fault with her work and Rutherford wanted to get her into his bed.

She felt her fear and sadness giving way to anger. Chris lifted her head and straightened her shoulders. Her tear-stained hands clenched into fists and she slammed them against the toilet bowl.

Chris was a good doctor, and she was a part of this staff. If people didn't like that, it was their problem, not hers! She was doing what she could to perform as a professional. She couldn't do anymore and she wouldn't.

She stood up and splashed her face with some cold water. Then she dried it on a towel. She didn't worry about ruining her make-up because she didn't wear any, at least at work.

Chris stared at herself in the mirror. Her eyes were a bit red and puffy from crying, but she couldn't do anything about that. It would go away in awhile. Still, if anyone who thought she shouldn't be in the hospital saw her, they would know she had been crying.

That was their problem, she reminded herself.

Chris left the bathroom. She had her rounds to complete.

4

Monday, March 16, 1936
7:58 p.m.

Jake walked into the Cumberland City Hall, an impressive stone-faced building built in 1911. The three-story building was supposed to be capped by a dome, but the City Fathers had decided it cost too much and left it off the finished building. Though the dome hadn't been built, the foundation for it was still on the roof of the building.

The police department was located in the basement of City Hall. Jake walked in the entrance, which was on the side of the building rather than up the stairs and through the atrium. He took off his raincoat and hung it on a hook just inside the door. Underneath, he was wearing his blue wool police uniform and badge.

The floor had huge and growing puddle of water on it from all of the hanging raincoats dripping dry. Jake walked over to his desk. It was one of many in the open room. Only about one-quarter of the desks were occupied on night shift, though.

"Don't even sit down, buddy," Lieutenant Paul Lewellen called across the room.

Lewellen was a short man, but he was built like a mountain. He was an ex-military man like Jake, but unlike Jake, Lewellen had seen very little action. Jake had been fighting in Europe while Lewellen had been training soldiers in the States to fight. Still, Lewellen was a good man to work with and Jake liked him.

"Come on, Lieutenant. It's raining out and it's late on a weeknight. There can't be something wrong already." Jake had been hoping that the rain would keep everyone in and it would be a quiet day. He wanted to work his shift, go home and stay as far away from water as possible.

"The rain's the problem," Lewellen said.

"How? I saw the Potomac when I came in. If it's beginning to rise, I didn't notice it."

Lewellen shook his head. "Not the Potomac. Wills Creek. I had a call that the folks in Locust Grove are putting up flood walls. That could be trouble."

Jake shrugged. "I think it's another false alarm. People are just antsy because we haven't had a flood in years. They think we're due."

The Rain Man

Jake knew the area was actually more than due, though he would not admit it. In the last century, Cumberland had had no less than eleven floods with the last one being in 1924. So, yes, they were long overdue for another flood, but Jake didn't think that the city would flood every time it rained.

But it is March.

Jake pushed the thought out of his mind.

"It's not my decision, Jake. Chief Eyerman wants us to keep an eye on things. He's one of those antsy people. Since you're the first one in, you get to go check it out. So just sign out a car and take a ride out to Locust Grove and take a look at things out there. If the creek's rising, even if it doesn't hit flood stage, we're going to have to let the people along the creek know so that they can clear out their basements," Lewellen said.

Jake rolled his eyes, but he nodded. "Yes, sir." At least the chief wasn't putting Jake on foot patrol this morning.

Jake walked down the hall to the desk sergeant who was also in charge of the vehicles. Bud Seeler was sitting behind his desk and reading yesterday's *Cumberland Daily News*. He couldn't afford the fifty cents a month to get his own copies so he always read whatever copies were left lying around the office from the day shift.

"What do you have available, Bud?" Jake asked.

"I've got your choice of motorcycles. I know you like them," Bud said as he folded the newspaper closed.

"Ha, ha. Very funny. I'd like a car, please."

"Take number four. It needs gas so stop and fill up before you go too far."

Bud tossed Jake the keys. Jake caught them in the air with barely a jingle. He walked into the garage and climbed into the Ford sedan. It was a small car, not designed to carry a lot of officers like the ones the police used to drive when they raided speakeasies during Prohibition.

The engine started up easily. The mechanic opened up the garage door for him. Jake waved to him as he pulled out into the rain.

He stopped at the Richfield station on his way out of town. It was near the intersection of Mechanic Street and Centre Street next to the American Oil Company. While the attendant filled up the gas tank, Jake walked behind the station and stood next to a 20,000-gallon cylindrical tank to look into Wills Creek.

The creek was high enough to cover the rocks in the streambed without causing ripples to mark where they were. The water was running fast, too, but it was still well below flood levels. Of course, the rain hadn't stopped yet. Jake just didn't want to imagine another flood.

He sighed and looked across the creek and up to the top of the mountains. There were still traces of snow here, which meant there would be more in the higher elevations. The rain had warmed up, too. It was warm enough to melt the snow. Whether it flooded or not would depend a lot on the snow pack. If it stayed frozen, things would probably be all right. If it melted during the rain, then there would probably be flooding to some degree.

Jake walked back around to the front of the building and paid the attendant for the gas. He pulled onto the National Road and headed through the Narrows, a gap between Wills and Haystack mountains just wide enough for the Baltimore and Ohio and Western Maryland Railroad tracks, the river and the highway to pass through.

He drove through the winding Narrows and turned right to cross the bridge over Wills Creek into Locust Grove. He pulled his car off to the side of the road. Locust Grove had flooded even more times than Cumberland had over the years, and being upriver from Cumberland, it also flooded first when Wills Creek was the cause of the flooding. Conditions in the small town would be a good indicator of what was coming for Cumberland.

People stood out in the rain filling sandbags and laying them along the river. Porch lights, lanterns and headlights from cars all provided light for the townspeople to work by. They were working together, and it looked like one row had been laid out along most of the creek bank.

Jake hoped that they were overreacting.

He turned off the engine and climbed out into the rain. Through the wet grass, he walked to where one group of people worked shoveling sand into a canvas bag. An old man stopped to look at Jake. The man was drenched, but he ignored the rain. He topped off the bag and nodded to the man holding it.

"Take it away," he said.

"Don't you think you're jumping the gun a bit, old timer?" Jake asked the man.

The white-haired man looked up at Jake and rolled his eyes. He spit a wad of chewing tobacco out and said, "I'd rather look foolish and have my house intact than to be sitting on the front porch saying there won't be no flood as the waters come over the bank and wash my house into Cumberland. I won't be looking foolish, though. I've lived here all my life. I know when it's going to flood and so does anyone else who's lived here long enough."

"It's only been raining an hour or so. How do you know it will flood?"

The old man snorted and tapped his shoulder. "I've got arthritis in the joint here. Had it for years. Whenever the weather changes, I can feel it coming a day, sometimes two, ahead of it happening. Over the years, I've been able to figure out how bad a storm will be by pain I feel. Twinges mean light storms. Sharp pains mean thunderstorms. A throbbing pain means heavy rains."

The man reminded Jake of Art and his knee. Maybe the two of them could compare pains and become weather forecasters.

"So what did you feel with this storm?" Jake asked.

The man frowned. "Constant, sharp pain."

"What's that mean?"

The man hefted the half-full bag. "What do you think it means, Sergeant?"

The Rain Man

Jake's eyebrows arched. "You mean you got all of these people to do this because of a pain in your shoulder?"

"My shoulder's never been wrong yet, which is more than I can say for those forecasts in the newspaper."

"But nothing's happened yet. The creek's not rising. The rain may stop."

"And I may become President of the United States, too." His expression indicated how likely he thought that would be. "I can't fill bags too quickly, not and cover all my waterfront in time if I wait until it's been raining for a day. We need to work together now. And I'll tell you something else." The man stomped hard on the ground. "The snow's beginning to melt, but the ground is still frozen. When the snow melts, it's going to run right off the mountains. The ground won't take it. So where do you think it will go?"

Jake considered that. It all came back to the snow. The snow would make the difference between high waters and flood waters if there was any appreciable amount of rain.

Jake suppressed a shudder. "Good luck then. I hope you're wrong, though."

The old man stared out over the creek and frowned. "I do, too."

Jake got back into the patrol car and headed back into town. Everyone seemed to think it was going to flood. They thought that Cumberland was due and this was the year. But they had thought it would flood once already this year and a few times last year, too. Nothing had come of those instances. Why should this storm be the one?

Because the snow was melting and there was a lot of it.

And it was March.

As Jake drove into town on Mechanic Street, he saw a man holding an umbrella run into the street and wave him over toward an alley. Jake turned into the alley and stopped his car.

A body was lying across the alley blocking the road.

The man ran up to the window. Jake rolled it down.

"That man's dead, officer. I was on my way into work and I saw him lying there like he was asleep," he said. He looked scared.

The man was middle-aged. That meant that he had probably missed the Great War, which meant that he wasn't used to seeing death.

Jake climbed out of the car.

"What's your name, sir?" Jake asked the man.

"Charles VanMeter."

"Tell me how you found the body, Mr. VanMeter," Jake said while he squatted down to stare at the dead man's head.

The dead man's eyes were wide open and staring into the rain. The left side of his head was oddly dented and matted with blood. Oddly enough, the man was lying on his back with his arms crossed over his chest. Someone had positioned him like that. He hadn't smashed his own head open and then lay down to die.

"I live on Franklin Street, but I'm a bookkeeper for the city. I walk this way to get home every evening. This evening when I walked through here, I found him lying there. I thought that he was drunk at first."

"Was there anybody else nearby when you found him?"

VanMeter shook his head. "Not that I saw."

Jake squatted down next to the body and looked around. The brick paving was too hard for a shoe to have left footprints and there wasn't anything out of the ordinary around the body.

"How did you know he was dead?" Jake asked.

"His head's caved in on the side. It's not natural. It doesn't take a doctor to figure out that means he's dead."

Jake sighed. This was not starting out to be a good shift for him.

"Did you touch him?" Jake asked VanMeter.

"No. I nearly threw up just looking at him," VanMeter said. He clutched at his umbrella with both hands as if it was a talisman that would protect him from whatever had killed the man in the street.

Jake stood up and circled the body slowly. Most of the blood had been washed away by the rain, making the crushed skull quite obvious.

The dead man had been murdered. It was obvious, but Jake was a bit surprised nonetheless. North Side wasn't known for being the rough area of town. That was a reputation reserved for Little Egypt on the other side of town.

There weren't even any bars nearby that might have contributed to a drunken brawl that had spilled out into the street.

Jake reached down and pulled the dead man's wallet from his pocket. There was still ten dollars in it. So robbery was apparently not the motive for the man's murder. Jake went through the rest of the items in the wallet. He found pictures of the man's family. He also found an identification card for the railroad.

"His name was Mark Connelly," Jake said, reading the identification.

Charles VanMeter shrugged. "That means nothing to me. I don't recognize him either. He's not from this neighborhood. I know everyone around here. I've lived in North Side all my life."

Jake stood up and looked around. The alley had two row homes on either side of it. One building didn't have windows that looked out onto the street. The other did. How could someone have been murdered here and no one hear anything? Hadn't there been sounds of a fight? Shouts? Grunts? Screams?

There were pink pools of water on the alleyway. So the man had bled here, which meant he most likely had also been murdered here. The man's body had been laid across the alley. Jake stared at the body. He had no idea what had happened, except that this man had seemingly been killed silently and without witnesses in a very brutal way.

The Rain Man

"Can I go now?" VanMeter asked. "I have to get to home. My wife will be wondering what happened to keep me so late."

Jake took VanMeter's address. VanMeter hurried out of the alley and walked north on Centre Street. Jake was sure the news of the murder would be all over town in a few hours. It would be spread among the politicians even quicker since the man worked for the city. Chief Eyerman would want the murder to be solved to put the politicians at ease and make himself look good. If possible, he would want it solved tonight so it wouldn't influence tomorrow's election.

Jake walked out the North Centre Street end of the alley to the first house that bordered it. This was the one that didn't have any windows that looked onto the alley. It was also abandoned as far as Jake could see. He looked in the front windows and all he saw was an empty room. He wondered if one of the banks had foreclosed on the home and kicked the family out on the street. There were too many empty homes in Cumberland because banks were struggling to survive the depression.

Jake crossed the alley and knocked on the door to the other house. There was no answer, but Jake thought he saw movement inside. He knocked again and this time he was louder.

An old man answered the door. The man was bald. His eyes were unusually large and gray. Tufts of white hair seemed to bulge from the man's ears.

"What can I do for you, officer?" the old man asked.

"I'm investigating a murder, sir."

The old man cupped his hand to his ear. "You'll have to speak up. I have some trouble hearing. The sound of all this rain falling in the background doesn't help either."

"May I use your phone, sir? I'm investigating a murder," Jake said loudly.

The old man looked startled. "A murder? Here?"

"In the alley," Jake said, jerking a finger in that direction.

The old man looked toward the alley as if he could see the body though the brick wall. Then he waved toward Jake. "Come in, officer. Come in."

Jake stepped inside to make the call to the coroner.

As he did, he realized that his hopes of a peaceful day had vanished with the setting sun.

5

Monday, March 16, 1936
8:47 p.m.

Jake was sitting in his car trying to get warm and dry when the ambulance pulled up with its siren wailing. Jake groaned. He had just been getting rid of the chill as some of the moisture on him dried. He climbed out of his warm car and was drenched in moments. Jake waved the ambulance attendants into the alley.

"You didn't have to rush, guys. This man's in no hurry, and the medical examiner's not here yet," Jake said.

"The doctor's on his way," the driver said. His name was Fred Snow. Jake knew everyone with the city fire companies because of his frequent contact with them.

"Of course, Dr. Rutherford's in no rush. We can't go anywhere until he clears the body," the other attendant, Gregory Frantz added.

The longer the medical examiner took to declare the body dead and collect any information he might want, the longer Jake would have to stand in the way and keep away spectators.

Dr. Vincent Rutherford, the medical examiner, pulled up behind the ambulance in his Ford coupe. He opened his umbrella and climbed out of the car.

Vincent was a handsome man, who kept his fingernails manicured and his black mustache trimmed. Chris said he was arrogant. Jake wasn't surprised. He thought that most doctors had a touch of arrogance, even Chris.

"How ya doin', Doc?" Jake said.

"I was looking forward to a quiet evening, Jake. I didn't get too much sleep last night," the doctor said.

Vincent squatted down to stare at the dead man's hands. He rubbed his chin while his eyes gleamed with excitement.

"Did you have a streak of luck?" Vincent was a poker lover who played wherever he could find a game going. He was also very good at cards. Jake had sat in on a few games with Vincent and always come out on the losing end.

The doctor nodded. "I finished up fifty dollars ahead."

"You probably took it from some poor fools who got hit with a frying pan by their wives when they got home for losing their pay," Jake commented.

Vincent shrugged. "That's what looks like happened to this poor guy." He touched the bloody head wound and pressed in on it. It gave too easily. What should have been solid skull moved as if it was loose tissue.

"Was he one of your poker buddies?" Jake asked.

Vincent looked over at him. "This guy? No." Vincent shook his head. "I've never seen him before, but then again, if he's not a beautiful woman, a funeral director or a poker player, I probably wouldn't. Don't you know who he is?"

Jake was always surprised at how small some people's circle of acquaintances was. Jake probably knew half the people in town from his work, but he always forgot that some jobs didn't allow people to circulate through town much.

"His railroad identification said his name is Mark Connelly, but that doesn't mean much to me."

"Well, if you don't know him, that says something. He might have been an out-of-towner. Maybe he was a hobo," Vincent suggested.

Jake shook his head. "He doesn't have the look. Besides, his driver's license had a Cumberland address. He lives over on Arch Street."

"Do we have pictures?"

"I took some before the ambulance arrived." Each of the police department's cars had a camera as well as other equipment that an officer might need at a crime scene stored in the trunk.

Vincent stood up. "Fine, let's get him to the hospital for an autopsy. I'll sign the death certificate there once I've had a closer look at his head."

Vincent turned, walked back to his car and drove off down Centre Street. Jake watched him go without so much as a goodbye.

Jake waved the ambulance attendants over.

Fred and Gregory hurriedly opened the rear of the ambulance. They pulled out a canvas stretcher and carried it over to the body. The two attendants lifted the dead man onto the stretcher.

"So the good doctor is going to dissect this guy?" Gregory said.

"We need to know how he was killed. Dr. Rutherford likes this sort of case. It makes him feel like a detective."

Gregory laughed and shook his head. "Detective, nothing. He's just looking for material to write his scholarly papers for journals."

The two men lifted the stretcher and loaded it into the rear of the ambulance. Gregory climbed in with it and Fred closed the doors.

"Stay dry," Fred told him.

He climbed in the front of the ambulance and drove off without the siren wailing. He waved to Jake as he drove down the alley to turn onto Mechanic Street.

A crowd had started to gather around the mouth of the alley with the appearance of the ambulance. Jake walked toward them and made eye contact with each person. He tried to remember what each person looked like. There was a chance that the murderer was in the crowd, watching to see what would happen with the body or if he was in danger of being identified.

"Did any of you see what happened here?" Jake asked loudly in an official tone.

A few people shook their heads. Most did nothing but stare at Jake as if he was speaking French. Nothing is more oblivious than a crowd.

Jake seriously doubted that he would find anything more here. The rain would wash away any clues if it hadn't already. He needed a lead on who might have wanted Mark Connelly dead. He was going to have to talk to the man's family and his co-workers and see what they would tell him.

Jake now knew what he would be doing for the rest of the night.

Lewellen would probably assign him to deliver the bad news to Mark Connelly's wife. Jake didn't look forward to doing that, but he had opened the case. He would see it through. Mrs. Connelly might even be able to help him with the investigation.

Jake climbed back into his squad car and drove south on Mechanic Street, passing Thompson Buick. He turned left on Baltimore Avenue and drove through the downtown business district and crossed over the B&O Railroad tracks. He made a right on Park Street, then left on Williams Street and followed it up a hill and through a residential area until he got to Memorial Hospital.

By the time he got to the four-story brick building, the ambulance attendants had already taken the body into the hospital. They would be taking it to the morgue, which is where Jake headed.

The morgue was located in the basement, which seemed a fitting location for such a creepy place. He walked in just as Fred and Gregory were transferring the body onto the porcelain examining table.

Vincent stood off to the side, staring at the body. He pulled on a pair of rubber gloves and set his tools on a table beside the body.

"Are you going to stay, Jake?" Vincent asked.

Jake shrugged, not wanting to stay at all. "I'd like to hear what your initial impressions are."

Vincent began to remove the man's clothes after first examining them. Mark Connelly wore overalls and a red flannel shirt. Vincent turned the shirt inside out and examined it under a magnifying glass.

"What was he doing in an alley between Centre and Mechanic if he lived in South Side?" Vincent asked.

Jake shrugged. "If I knew that, I'd probably have a better idea of how he was killed. What can you tell me?"

Vincent moved the large magnifying glass and studied the side of Connelly's head. Vincent used a set of tweezers to pick bits of bone and stone out of Connelly's hair. He dropped the small pieces into a tray on the edge of the examining table. Jake looked away to keep from gagging. He would never be so blase' about death, he told himself, not even if he had served in a dozen wars.

"The head wound was certainly enough to kill him," Vincent said. "Odd though."

"Odd how?" Jake was grasping for a clue. Anything would help.

"Was there a brick or hammer nearby?"

Jake shook his head. "No. Judging from the blood on the street, I thought someone had slammed his head against the street again and again."

Vincent nodded. "That's what it looks like to me. The area where the skull is broken is broad and even. I thought it could have been a brick, or perhaps, a large hammer."

"But?"

"But, if you were going to kill someone by smashing his head against the street, wouldn't it be easier to do it back and forth rather than side to side?"

Vincent demonstrated what he meant by shaking Jake by the shoulders. Jake immediately saw the difference. By smashing Mark Connelly's head against the street sideways, Connelly's shoulder would have been in the way and broken the momentum. It was easier for him to slam the man's head backwards. So what was the point of crushing the side of Mark Connelly's head instead of the back?

"How could the killer have done it that way?" Jake asked.

Vincent shrugged. "I've just started examining him. He may have been stabbed and then fell, striking his head, but I doubt it."

"Why's that?"

"Because there are pieces of brick embedded in his skull. He wouldn't have gotten that simply from falling. Either his head was slammed repeatedly against the brick road to get the brick embedded in his head or he fell from atop a building."

"He didn't fall," Jake said simply.

"I can see that. His skull's the only thing that's broken. If the impact had been enough to bust his head, it would have also busted a few other bones."

"He also wouldn't have fallen in a way that made him look like he was laid out in a funeral parlor," Jake added.

Vincent didn't seem surprised, but then very little seemed to surprise him. He was very familiar with death in its various forms.

"So what you have here is a man who was probably murdered in a fit of rage," Jake surmised.

"Why do you say that?" Vincent asked.

"Well, if the murder had been premeditated, wouldn't the murderer have used a weapon? It would have been easier, say, if he had a loose brick with him to smash Connelly's head in. The positioning of the body also indicates that the murderer probably had some regret over what he had done."

"You sound like a psychologist."

Jake shrugged. "I've just worked with people for a long time. Every cop has to be a bit of a psychologist, especially those of us who walk a beat. How long do you think it will take until you finish the autopsy?"

"Probably not too long. Maybe an hour or so. I can call you at the station when I finish up," Vincent told him.

Jake nodded. "That's fine. I've got to stop by his home to tell his wife or family about this. Plus, I'll begin questioning whoever I can find there."

Jake left the morgue and walked upstairs. He started for the front door of the hospital, but paused before he went outside. He turned down the hall and asked the nurse on duty if Dr. Evans was around.

The Rain Man

"I saw her in the doctors' lounge," the nurse told him.

Jake walked down the hallway and pushed open the door to the doctors' lounge. Chris was inside writing some notes into a file.

"Hi there, beautiful," he said.

Chris looked up and brushed back a strand of loose red hair over her ear. She smiled when she saw him.

"That's Dr. Beautiful to you," she told him with mock seriousness.

"Good evening, Dr. Beautiful. I'm surprised to see you still here."

He walked inside and sat down across the table from her.

"I have a few serious patients I wanted to check on before I went home. What are you doing up here?" she asked as she closed the file.

"I'm working on a murder investigation."

"Murder?"

Jake nodded. "The ambulance just brought the body in a little while ago. I was downstairs with Vincent. He's trying to discover the dead man's secrets."

Chris frowned briefly.

"Do you have the murderer?" she asked.

Jake shook his head. "And the prospects don't look so good right at the moment. It's already beginning to look like an odd case."

Chris laid a hand on his arm. "You'll figure it out. You just have to get enough information, which I'm sure you'll have before too long."

"I hope so. I don't want this hanging over my head when we go on vacation."

"Jake, about that vacation…"

Jake smiled. "It's going to be great. I'm really looking forward to it."

He forced himself to act happier than he felt. He had to keep up a positive front or Chris would find a way to back out of the trip.

Chris sighed and said, "So am I."

6

Monday, March 16, 1936
8:51 p.m.

It took Raymond more than an hour to walk across town to where his room was located on Virginia Avenue at the B&O Railroad YMCA. The rain soaked him to the skin because he had no umbrella or even a hat. It hadn't been raining when he had finished work at the funeral home. Maybe it was a different night. Maybe the Rain Man had controlled him for a full day, though even a few minutes had been too long given what had happened in the alley.

Drivers passing by in their dry cars didn't stop to offer him a ride. In fact, a few of them splashed him, which soaked any spot on him that the rain might have missed.

Raymond didn't get angry and shake a fist at the drivers, though. He had more important things on his mind. He tried to recall what he had done during the time between leaving work and finding himself in the North Side alley, but the hours eluded him, hidden by the Rain Man. Raymond needed to recover that lost time.

What if he had met the dead man in Johnny's Place? What if someone had noticed Raymond leaving with the dead man?

Raymond couldn't remember anything after he had left work. The time belonged to the Rain Man. Raymond was simply the body that the Rain Man had chosen to use.

The Rain Man just laughed, which only made the pain in his head feel worse. Raymond rubbed the left side of his head where the pain was the worst, although it would do no good. It never did. Raymond could feel the knotted scar tissue and his odd-shaped skull.

By the time he reached the YMCA, Raymond felt as if he had just climbed out of the bathtub. The rain ran down his face and into his eyes, making it hard for him to see. He still wore his work suit, but it clung to him and weighed him down.

His suit!

36

The Rain Man

That should tell him something. He must have gone right from his job at the Wolford Funeral Home to...where?

He hadn't gone to his room or he would have changed out of the suit to keep it clean. He had gone somewhere else between South Liberty Street where the funeral home was located and the YMCA. Where?

It was hard to concentrate with all the rain falling. Raymond could feel each individual raindrop hit him. Each drop seemed to explode against his head. With each strike, the pain spread just a little bit further around his skull.

Why couldn't the rain just end? Why couldn't he be left in peace... sweet painless peace? Wasn't that what the Rain Man promised in exchange for obedience? Raymond had obeyed, whether he had wanted to or not, so why didn't he feel relief?

I am the Rain Man! This is my element! I will not be denied! the Rain Man raged.

Raymond put his hands on the side of his head in the vain hope to block out the Rain Man's voice. He felt his blood pounding just beneath his skin. It matched the rhythm of the raindrops on his head.

The pink scar tissue from his war wounds tingled as if it was electrically charged. Raymond had never seen what the scars looked like, but he could feel them. The pain always came from his scars.

Because hair wouldn't grow from the scarred area, Raymond grew his brown hair longer so that it hung over the multitude of scars on the side of his head. The wounds still caused his head to look slightly lopsided, and it gave the barbers a fit when they tried to cut his hair to make it look even.

If only he could fight the pressure that caused the pain...

He could simply squeeze the pain away between his hands.

Raymond pressed inward and felt a slight relief from the pain. He pushed harder.

Maybe the Rain Man was right. To free himself from the pain would take drastic action. He could only find freedom as the man in the alley had this morning.

Yes, yes, the Rain Man encouraged him. *Imagine how good your life will be once you are free from the pain.*

Raymond eyed the brick corner of a nearby building. It was sharp and hard. It could serve to do the job that the exploding shell in France hadn't been able to do. Could Raymond run hard enough to bring permanent relief to his pain?

Yes! That will serve. Be free of the pain, Raymond. Do it. DO IT!

Raymond stared at the rough, square edge and nodded his head. It would be so easy. It would be a moment of pain no greater than he already felt at times, and then he would no longer feel any pain.

No!

He clenched his eyes shut, ran to the wooden stairs and quickly climbed to the front porch of the YMCA. He stopped there and leaned back against the wooden boards of the wall, gasping. When he straightened up, he noticed the puddle of water at his feet. He was shedding the rain.

Coward, the Rain Man scolded.

Raymond calmed himself and walked into the lobby of the YMCA. It was brightly lit with wall and ceiling lamps. A half a dozen men sat around a large table, smoking and playing cards.

Gary, the desk clerk, looked up from the copy of the *Cumberland Evening News* that he was reading. His eyes ran from Raymond's head to the floor and he frowned.

"Look at the mess you're making. I'll have to mop it up," he said.

"What day is it?" Raymond asked.

"What day? Have you been drinking again, Raymond?"

Raymond hurried over to the front desk and slapped his hands on the counter. "What day is it!"

"It's Monday, you drunk!" Gary snapped.

"I'm not drunk."

"Then I guess you're just an idiot who walks around without a raincoat and doesn't know what day it is."

Raymond turned away and trudged up the stairs to the third floor, leaving a water trail behind him. He might not be a drunk, but he certainly wasn't going to tell Gary that he was a murderer.

The B&O Railroad YMCA had four floors with the lobby on the second floor. The building used to be the Eutaw House back about the time Raymond had been born. Back then, it had thirty-one bedrooms, a restaurant, a pool room and a bar. Then the B&O Railroad bought the building in 1905 and the bar became storage rooms and toilets.

Raymond pulled his keys from his pocket, which was no easy feat. The wet fabric in his pants clung to Raymond's hand preventing him from reaching them. He finally fished them out and opened his door.

Raymond rushed inside, but he shut the door quietly behind him because he didn't want to make the pain in his head worse.

He stripped out of his saturated suit and shirt and hung them over the radiator to drip dry. He laid a towel under the radiator to catch the water. Then Raymond put on his robe. It was warm because he had draped it over the radiator before he had left for work last night. He could remember that much at least.

Raymond's room, like the other rooms in the YMCA, had a bed in one corner, a high bureau, a closet, a desk and chair and shelves above the desk. There were two windows in the room. Between the windows was a nightstand with a pitcher and bowl on it. He used the water in the pitcher to wash up when he didn't want to go down the hallway to one of the common bathrooms.

He took the bottle of aspirin off the shelf and quickly downed four tablets without any water. They usually didn't help the pain, but then the pain usually wasn't this bad. He was willing to try anything if it had a chance of stopping, or at least easing, his pain.

Raymond started a pot of coffee with yesterday's coffee grounds. It wouldn't be as good as fresh coffee, but Raymond had to be careful with his money. He wouldn't get paid again until Friday night.

He had a small cook stove that he used to heat the water in his room. He wasn't supposed to have it because of the danger of starting a fire, but he wasn't supposed to have other things in his room that he had. Compared to them, an open flame was a minor concern.

Raymond cut two slices of day-old bread off a loaf and buttered them. He needed some food in his stomach. His hunger was probably one of the reasons the pain in his head felt so bad. Maybe a meal in his stomach would make the pain bearable. He would eat and then he would go to bed. Hopefully, when he awakened in the afternoon, the rain would have ended and the pain would be gone.

Raymond ate the bread and was still hungry. He took an apple from a fruit basket on his desk and ate that, too.

Outside, the rain beat a steady rhythm on his windows. It seemed as if it was hammering to get inside the room. It wanted to hurt him.

Why couldn't it stop? Without the rain, the Rain Man had no power over him. Raymond touched the window pane with his fingertips. He could feel the glass vibrating under the rain's assault.

"God, please make the rain stop," Raymond whispered.

He closed his eyes and counted to ten. When he opened them again, the rain was still coming down. He didn't know why he bothered to pray when God never answered his prayers.

Because I am your god, Raymond, and I want it to rain, the Rain Man rumbled inside his head.

"No!" Raymond screamed.

He slammed his fist into the wall next to the window. He wasn't a large man, but his anger gave him strength. The plaster cracked and a small chunk fell to the floor, exposing the lathe behind it.

Raymond struck the wall again, making the crack even larger. Some of the wooden slats of the lathe cracked. A small cloud of plaster dust floated in the air.

He hit it again and this time his knuckles bled. Raymond screamed in pain. It wasn't from pain in his hands, but the pain in his head.

He grabbed handfuls of hair and nearly pulled them out. He would have if he thought it would ease his pain, but he knew that it wouldn't.

Only one thing would ease his pain.

The Rain Man.

But Raymond didn't want to let the Rain Man control him. He had seen what happened when the Rain Man promised to ease his pain. The Rain Man only brought him a different type of pain.

Raymond screamed again. He grabbed a picture of his Allegany County High School senior class from off the wall. The class of 1917 stood outside of a building that had burned down years ago. Raymond flung the picture across the room. It smashed into the far wall and the glass shattered in a poor imitation of the rain.

Good. I can use your anger to ease the pain, the Rain Man told him.

"No!" Raymond yelled.

He ran the half a dozen steps across the room and fell to his knees across the glass shards. He picked up the picture and tossed it off to the side. The picture was not important. The glass was.

He found a large triangular piece that was pointed in a wicked hook on one end. It would serve well. He held it against his wrist.

No, that is not the way. Let me show you.

Raymond knew the way to end the pain. It was the only way he could stop his pain for good and be free of the Rain Man forever.

He smiled as he pressed the glass hook on the end of the glass into his wrist. He felt a moment of intense pain, like a bomb going off inside his head.

Then the world turned black.

7

Monday, March 16, 1936
8:57 p.m.

Chris was on the third floor west wing of Memorial Hospital and nearly finished her evening rounds. She had calmed down from the incident with Vincent Rutherford by concentrating on her patients and making sure they were comfortable. The short visit from Jake had helped, too. She had wanted to tell him what had happened with Rutherford but had settled instead for small talk even if it had been about camping at Swallow Falls.

She came out of John Hightower's room on the second floor after telling him that he was ready to be discharged. Hightower worked with the WPA and had caught pneumonia working outdoors in bad weather. William Finn, the hospital superintendent, stopped her in the hall and glared at her.

"I've been looking for you, Dr. Evans," Finn said.

"I've been making my rounds," Chris told him.

She was surprised to still see him at the hospital. She wondered what had happened to keep him here so late in the evening.

The superintendent nodded. "Among other things. I need to speak with you in my office."

"I'll be down when I'm finished my rounds. I shouldn't be long."

Finn raised his eyebrows. "No. I need to talk to you now." His voice was firm and brooked no dissent, but Chris being who she was had to try.

"But I…"

"Now," Finn said sharply.

He turned and walked toward the elevator at the intersection of the two hallways. Chris sighed and followed him. What had she done to anger him now?

They rode down in the elevator together, but neither one said anything. Finn stared at the floor numbers changing. Chris looked at the

41

front of the elevator. The door slid open and Chris followed Finn down the hall and into his office in one corner of the first floor. It was at least six times larger than the office Chris occupied on Second Street in South Cumberland.

"Close the door, please," he said as he sat down behind his desk.

She did so and sat down in an overstuffed chair across the desk from him. Through the window behind him, Chris could see that it was still raining outside.

Finn steepled his fingers in front of his face and stared at her. She stared back not wanting to show weakness in front of him. She laid her hands in her lap and waited for Finn to speak.

"I know you have certain ideas about a woman's role in society, doctor. Your ideas have led you to even be deceptive at times, but it does not give you leave to go about attacking your colleagues because they disagree with you or question your ability," Finn said.

"I don't understand," Chris said.

Finn leaned forward. "No? Do you realize that Dr. Rutherford is currently lying on the couch in his office with ice on his groin? What you did to him was an excessive reaction simply because he questioned your diagnosis on a patient. You're lucky that he wasn't permanently hurt."

Chris was shocked. She hadn't thought that Rutherford would say anything about the incident in the supply closet, let alone paint himself as the victim. She'd thought that his ego from being rejected would have silenced him. Chris knew for a fact that Rutherford wasn't lying on the couch with an ice pack between his legs, though she wished it was true. Jake had been down to the morgue and hadn't mentioned anything about Rutherford lying down. He surely would have said something if he'd seen anything as unusual as a doctor nursing his groin with an ice pack. Jake hadn't even said whether Rutherford was limping or not.

"That's not why I kneed him," Chris said.

Finn slapped his hand on the desk. "I don't care why you did it! It's unacceptable. You are a doctor not a street brawler."

"He deserved it. He pulled me into the supply closet and tried to grope me."

Finn stared at her in amazement. His eyes bulged slightly and his mouth hung open. "I am sure that you exaggerate. Dr. Rutherford has been a member of this staff far longer than you have. If such conduct was common from him, I'm sure I would have heard of it by now."

Only if he bothered to listen to hospital gossip, which he didn't.

"I didn't say anything about it being commonplace, though you seem to think that it might be," Chris defended herself.

"I don't think it is. Dr. Rutherford is a gentleman."

"That's because the nurses are too afraid to say anything."

Finn sighed and shook his head. "Or maybe it's that nothing like you describe happens with either you or the nurses. Dr. Rutherford's conduct has always been professional, exemplary even. That's more than I can say about how you've conducted yourself," Finn said.

Chris tried to keep from screaming, though it was what she wanted to do. How dare this man question her honesty and professionalism!

"Just because you don't like me, sir, doesn't mean that I'm wrong all of the time," Chris said more sharply than she had intended.

Finn waved a finger at her. "See, you make this personal when it is not. I am not saying you are wrong all the time. I am saying that you are wrong this time."

"No, you are saying that in an instance when it is my word against Dr. Rutherford's, you are going to believe Dr. Rutherford."

"One of you is wrong. You both are telling two different stories. His assertions are more believable than yours, and if you were the victim, as you contend, why didn't you come to me and tell me your side of the story?" Finn asked.

"Because I thought that I had settled the situation on my own."

Finn sighed and held up a sheet of paper. "This incident report will be going into your personnel file. I would recommend that you not let your temper and opinions get the better of you again or more drastic actions will have to be taken. That will be all."

Chris stood up and headed for the door. She stopped there and turned back to Finn.

"Dr. Rutherford said I was upset with him because he questioned my treatment of one of my patients," Chris said.

Finn nodded. "Yes."

"Ask him which patient he spoke about and what the problem is. He won't be able to tell you. Then come tell me I'm a liar."

Chris left before Finn could reply. She didn't know if he would question Rutherford or not. It didn't matter. What mattered is that he was much more willing to believe what Rutherford told him about her.

She stalked down the hallway to the doctors' lounge, daring anyone to speak to her. She hadn't gone to Finn with her problems with Rutherford because she hadn't wanted to appear weak to him. Instead, he had used her independence against her as proof of her guilt.

Her face was red with barely concealed anger. Most of the people who saw her would assume it was caused by embarrassment at being dressed down by Finn.

Well, at least Rutherford was hurting. No, — she corrected herself — he wasn't hurting. Not yet at least.

In the lounge, she drank a cup of water and paced her anger out.

Calmed, she went back up to the second floor to finish her rounds. She no longer felt as calm as she had felt earlier and she struggled to find it once again. She could use another visit from Jake. She needed to talk to him. She needed someone to believe her.

When Chris finished her rounds, she went back to the lounge to get her raincoat and umbrella so she could go home. As she walked in, she saw Rutherford sitting in the chair. He smiled when he saw her.

"Get out," she said.

He shook his head. "I don't think so. This is the doctors' lounge, and after all, I am a doctor." He waved her into the lounge so that the door would close. "And I don't think you can do a thing about it. I understand Dr. Finn talked to you."

"He did," she admitted.

"Then I guess you know how things stand."

Rutherford stood up slowly and walked over to stand in front of her. He quickly kissed her. She raised her hand to slap him, but Rutherford wiggled his finger in her direction.

"Uh, uh, uh. You wouldn't want to get in trouble with Dr. Finn, would you?"

Chris crossed her arms under her breasts.

"Leave me alone before I scream," she threatened.

Rutherford faked a shiver. "Oooh, will the tough, independent female doctor actually show her weakness and scream? What would everyone think about her? She's just overreacting. She's just being a female. Why should she be afraid of a wounded man like the good Dr. Rutherford?"

Rutherford chuckled. Then he stepped around her toward the door.

"We'll get together again, sweetheart, when I'm feeling more up to it. That's a promise," Rutherford said.

It sounded more like a threat to Chris.

8

Monday, March 16, 1936
9:39 p.m.

Jake parked his patrol car on Arch Street and stepped out into the rain. It hit him like someone throwing a bucket of water in his face. He paused momentarily to wonder if it was heavier than it had been earlier this morning. If it kept up, they were going to need boats to get around the Queen City by the end of the tomorrow.

The image sent a shiver through Jake.

He hurried onto the porch of the brick duplex and knocked on the door. After a few moments, a woman opened the door. She was young in age, maybe twenty-five, but she looked at least twenty years older. She had a perpetual weariness around her green eyes. It was an expression Jake had grown used to seeing in recent years. More and more people had it. It was the expression of someone who was losing the fight against life and giving into despair. This woman was living in a day-to-day existence brought on by the Great Depression.

The woman looked at Jake's uniform and then brushed a wisp of stray brown hair out of her eyes. She held the collar of her robe close to her throat.

"So what did Mark do?" she asked.

"Excuse me?" Jake said.

An orange tabby cat ran past the woman's feet to get outside the house. Then it saw the rain pouring down and stopped. The woman bent down, picked up the cat and shooed it back inside the house.

When she stood up, she said, "I know I haven't done anything wrong so you're not here for me. My husband hasn't come home tonight so I figure he got himself into trouble." She didn't sound angry just resigned to the fact that her life had just changed.

At least Jake knew he was at the right place.

"I'm Sergeant Fairgrieve, ma'am. Does your husband get in trouble often?" Jake asked, hoping for some clue to what had happened to

Mark Connelly in that dark alley.

She shrugged. "Not often, I guess, but too often for me if you know what I mean."

Jake nodded. "Yes, ma'am, I guess I do, and I am here about your husband." He paused, wondering if there was an easy way to tell her this. "He's dead, ma'am."

The woman closed her eyes and sucked in a deep breath. When she opened her eyes, they were glossy with unshed tears.

"I think you'd better come in, Sergeant," she said.

She opened the door wider and Jake walked inside. The living room was sparsely decorated, but the furniture the Connellys did have was in good condition. The walls were painted, not wallpapered. Few pictures hung on them. The room was dimly lit with two table lamps on end tables at either end of the sofa. Times might be tough for the Connellys, but they were doing better than most. They still had a well-kept home.

Mrs. Connelly sat down on the red sofa and Jake sat on a hard chair across from her. He was near the radiator and could feel the warmth as it heated the air around it.

"What happened?" Mrs. Connelly asked.

"I don't know all the details yet, ma'am, but your husband's death will be investigated as a murder. His body was found earlier this morning in an alley in North End."

"North End? What was he doing over there?"

"I was hoping that you could tell me about that, Mrs. Connelly. Your husband's body was found in an alley between Mechanic and Centre Streets. Is there any reason he would have been over there?"

Mrs. Connelly shook her head. "He rarely went into North End. The only times we ever went there was when we needed to take National Highway to Frostburg or Garrett County."

"Do you know where your husband would have gone this evening?"

She only had to think a moment before she said, "Well, he would have been at work until five o'clock. If he's not home by five-thirty, then I know that means he's gone out for a few drinks with the men he works with. He's usually home by eight o'clock on those nights."

"And he didn't come home by eight tonight."

She nodded.

"When that has happened before, what did it mean?" Jake asked.

The Rain Man

"A few times it meant Mark passed out at a friend's house. Sometimes his friend called to let me know, sometimes not. Other times, it meant that you had him," Mrs. Connelly said. Jake understood "you" to mean "police."

Jake made a mental note to check the police files on Mark Connelly when Jake got back to the station to see if there was any information on the dead man.

"How many times has it been the police who had your husband?" He wondered if Mark couldn't hold his liquor and became a trouble-maker when he was drunk.

She thought for a moment. "About a dozen."

"For general drunkenness?"

Mrs. Connelly nodded. "Two times he got into a bar fight after he got drunk, and three times he was caught in a speakeasy raid before that foolishness ended. The rest of the times it was just because he got too loud and rowdy, but no one was ever hurt."

With so many arrests, Jake was surprised that he hadn't run across Mark Connelly before now. Jake had been with the police department since he got out of the army.

"Did your husband have a temper?"

"Only when he was drunk, but not that often because he usually didn't get drunk. He had to be really depressed or thinking money looked good coming in to go out drinking that much. It was why it didn't happen a lot. He hasn't made it home only about two dozen times over six or seven years," Mrs. Connelly explained.

Jake patted her hand. "I understand. Did your husband know anybody in North End? One of his drinking friends who he might have been going to see?"

Mrs. Connelly shook her head. "He never talked about knowing anyone over there. He worked for the railroad at the turntable so most of the people he knows and drinks with are other railroaders."

"Is there anyone your husband ever mentioned who he didn't like or who he thought didn't like him?" Jake asked, groping for leads.

"You mean who didn't like him enough to kill him?"

"Anyone, ma'am." Jake tried to keep the pleading tone out of his voice. He wanted to close this case quickly so Chief Eyerman wouldn't be after him to make an arrest.

Mrs. Connelly thought for awhile and then said, "Not really. He would say occasionally, 'Steve's an idiot' or talk about an argument he had, but then he would be on good terms with that person the next day. Mark was a likable guy. Everybody thought so."

Someone didn't. Jake bit his lip to keep from saying it, though.

He pursed his lips. He wasn't getting too far with this questioning. His training and limited experience in this area told him that most murders had obvious perpetrators. He wasn't seeing one here. Why had Mark Connelly been in the north end of town? Who would want to kill him?

"What bars did your husband like to visit?"

"Johnny's Place. That's the only one he talked about. It's between here and the rail yard so it's a popular place for railroaders to stop," Mrs. Connelly told him.

Jake nodded. "I know the place. It's on Virginia Avenue."

"What am I going to do now? How am I going to get by without Mark's pay?" she asked. The orange cat began to walk in and out between her legs.

"Do you have family in town you can call, ma'am?" Jake asked.

She stopped walking and looked at him. "No, my family is all in Charleston."

She started pacing again.

"What about friends?" Jake continued.

"They're probably asleep."

"Should I call them anyway?"

She shook her head. "No, no. What am I going to do now?"

"I guess you'll need to get a job, Mrs. Connelly."

She stood up and began pacing back and forth across the living room. The cat followed her like a shadow. "Doing what?"

Jake shrugged. "I guess that is up to you, ma'am."

Jake stood up. He was finished here and Mrs. Connelly was beginning to ask questions that only she could find the answers to. Jake had changed her life, and now he would leave her to deal with it.

"Mark had a small insurance policy. I'll have to find that. I think Mark kept it in the bottom drawer of his dresser with the other important papers," Mrs. Connelly said out loud.

"Why don't you do that, Mrs. Connelly? I'm sure that should be able to get you through a year or two," Jake suggested.

"Is that all?" She seemed surprised that it wouldn't take care of her for the rest of her life.

Jake shrugged. "I don't really know. I'm just guessing."

The Rain Man

Jake left when she went upstairs to rummage though her husband's box of important papers. The rain was still coming down as he drove to Virginia Avenue and south to the B&O rail yard.

He parked in front of the main office and went inside to report to the manager that Mark Connelly was dead. Jake absent-mindedly wondered if the company would fill the now-open position or absorb it to save a little bit more money during this economic depression. Not surprisingly, the manager said the company would absorb the job.

As Jake walked from the office to the turntable, he saw a hobo slip off one of the freight cars of a waiting train and disappear into the shadows. That would be one more person looking for work in town or maybe the hobo would jump on the next train heading in a direction he liked. Cumberland was becoming filled with hobos because the train hub of two railroads was here. Some days, the city jail was filled with hobos if the railroad bull was having a particularly productive day in rounding them up and bringing them into the station.

Most of the hobos were harmless. They were men out of work who were looking for jobs, but there were some who were on the run because of other problems. Those were the ones that worried Jake.

Since Connelly had worked for the railroad, Jake wondered if the dead man had stumbled across a violent hobo. While Jake had heard of such things happening, the murders always happened near the rail yards. Why would Mark Connelly have gone somewhere with a hobo? And if it had been a hobo who had killed Connelly, why hadn't the hobo also robbed him?

That was key. The motive for the murder hadn't been money. Connelly's money had been in his wallet along with his identification.

It probably hadn't been a planned murder either since no weapon had been used to kill Connelly. It seemed to have been a crime of anger, but why had the murderer been angry and why had the anger been directed at Mark Connelly if he was a likable guy?

If Jake could just know why Mark had been murdered, he could narrow down the list of suspects from just about everyone in Cumberland.

He watched the turntable rotate into position. A worker came out and locked the tracks on the turntable to the regular tracks then waved to the engineer. A gray locomotive engine slowly rolled off the turntable and onto the track.

Jake walked over to the worker. He was about five inches taller than Jake was and, given the man's wide shoulders, maybe even five inches wider. His thick glasses had rainwater running down the lenses.

"My name's Jake Fairgrieve with the Cumberland Police," Jake introduced himself. He held out his hand and the man shook it.

"Did the bull collar a few more hobos tonight? I always thought he stayed inside when it rained," the worker said. Bull was slang for a railroad detective.

"I'm not here about the hobos. I'm looking for people who worked with Mark Connelly."

The man's eyebrows arched. "I work with him sometimes. What's the problem? He cause trouble at Johnny's Place again?"

Jake shook his head. "He was killed last night."

The man stopped walking and turned to face Jake. "Killed? What happened?"

"That's what I want to know. He was murdered in North End last night."

"What was Mark doing in North End?"

"That's another question I'd like to know the answer to. Do you have any idea why he would have been up that way? Did he have friends or family or a girlfriend?"

The worker snorted. "He was married."

"He wouldn't be the first man to have a girlfriend on the side," Jake noted.

"That's for rich men who can afford it. Mark's money either went home or to bartenders. Besides, he loved his wife. I don't know about family or friends, but I've never known him once to mention anybody who he visited living in North End.

The man shrugged and started walking again. Jake followed him.

"How well did you know Mark Connelly?" Jake asked.

"Well enough. We work...worked together on the turntable, maybe a week a month when our shifts matched up."

"And your name is?"

"Steve Laughton."

Was this the Steve Mrs. Connelly had mentioned her husband complaining about? This man did seem truly surprised at Connelly's death.

"What kind of person was he?" Jake asked.

"I've only known him to miss work twice in three years, at least that's what he said. Both times he was sick or at least he said he was." Laughton shrugged. "Maybe he was just sick of working. I've seen him drunk more times than I can count. He would be hungover, but he could still work."

"How was he when he was drunk?" Jake asked.

"Usually sleeping."

"How about when he was awake? Did he have a temper? Was he hard to work with?"

Laughton shrugged. "Not really. He took his time doing things, but he didn't make too many mistakes. Sometimes I got tired of waiting for him to catch up all of the time."

"So he got along with everyone he met."

Laughton shrugged again. "Basically. Some of the bartenders around town might have gotten a little angry with him from time to time when he fell behind on his bar tabs, but he always made it up and smoothed things over. He even paid for damage he caused in the bars."

Jake could sense that this conversation was going nowhere fast. Connelly was Mr. Nice Guy who nobody would kill, but someone did. Jake thanked Laughton for his time and headed back to his car.

He sat in his car staring at a train pulling out of the rail yard heading east. He felt like he was getting nowhere in finding out who had killed Mark Connelly. That made Jake uncomfortable. He didn't like knowing a murderer was roaming town and would most likely go free unless Jake got a lead in this case.

Mark Connelly might not have been a troublemaker, but no one seemed particularly upset that he was dead either.

No one but Jake and that was reason enough to find the murderer.

9

Monday, March 16, 1936
10:10 p.m.

Jake parked his black squad car a couple blocks from Johnny's Place in front of Cumberland Electric on Virginia Avenue. He didn't want to frighten anyone away from the bar by stopping right in front of it. Though Prohibition had been lifted, some people still worried every time they saw a police officer near a bar.

He walked up the street in the rain and paused under the large green awning that shaded the front of the bar. "Johnny's Place Cocktails and Liquor" was painted on the large front window. During Prohibition, the window had read "Johnny's Place for Lunch and Dinner." Police had raided it at least half a dozen times for selling liquor illegally during the 1920's. Now the bar made no pretensions about what it was.

Jake looked through the window into the dim interior of the bar. He saw two men sitting at the bar and no one at the tables. It was rainy and a weekday night; neither one of which helped business.

Jake walked inside the bar. He shook the rain off of himself and hung up his rain slicker. Then he took a seat at the bar a few stools down from the other men. To still be drinking at this hour meant those men were serious drinkers who weren't in the bar for conversation, particularly with a cop.

The bartender was an old man with a thin, white beard and mustache and no hair on top of his head. He wore a dingy white shirt and black trousers.

"Are you Johnny?" Jake asked.

"That'd be me, Sergeant."

"I'm trying to find out some information about a murder, Johnny."

Johnny stepped back from the bar. "What's that got to do with me? I run a respectable place here. Ain't been a fight for about a month and never a murder."

Johnny had a low standard for what was respectable.

"Do you know Mark Connelly?"

"Sure, he comes in here two or three times a week," Johnny answered quickly.

"Was he in here tonight?"

Johnny nodded. "Sure, I think I remember seeing him. We're a lot busier earlier in the evening when most people get off work, but if he had a drink I would have seen him, and Mark Connelly never has more than just one drink."

Jake knew that couldn't be true; not if Mark had been arrested for drunken rowdiness.

"What time did you see him?" Jake asked.

Johnny frowned. "I guess he came in here around five o'clock. No, he doesn't get off work until five so it had to be a little later than that. Maybe five-thirty."

Jake finally felt like he was beginning to make some headway. Connelly had finished his shift today and come here for a drink.

"When was the last time you remember seeing him?" Jake asked.

"Maybe six-thirty or so. He tends not to stay late on work nights. He needs the time to sleep off whatever he drinks here."

Now Jake had the beginnings of a trail. Maybe he could follow it until it ran out and that would help him know where to look for Mark's killer. He'd narrowed the gap to about an hour and a half of Mark's life that Jake had to account for.

"Was he with anyone when you saw him?" Jake asked.

"Sure. He was with the railroading group that always hangs out here after the end of their shift. They usually fill up the tables in the corner and that was where Mark was."

Jake wondered if it would be worth checking out each man in that group individually. It would be a lot of work, but it might come to that point if he wanted to close this case successfully.

He looked over at the two men sitting further down the bar in the shadows. "They look like they'll stay until you close," he noted.

Johnny shrugged. "The depression bogs some men down and they need relief, and I'm not talking about the government's idea of relief."

"I'm guessing if they need that much relief, they probably need the money they're spending on drinks to give them some relief."

Johnny straightened up to his full height as if he had been offended. "I guess it's up to them to decide how to spend it seeing as how it's theirs."

Jake nodded. "Do you have any soda pop? I'm thirsty."

"I have Coca-Cola and ginger ale for mixed drinks."

"I'll take a Coke."

Johnny drew the soda pop from a fountain and slid it in front of Jake. Jake took a deep swig and looked at the two men at the other end of the bar again. He was looking at one man's profile and the other man had his head lowered so that Jake couldn't make out any of his features. The man whose profile he was looking at was familiar, though.

Where had he seen him before?

"Ray?" Jake said.

The man turned to look at him. His eyes had dark circles under them and his face was drawn as if he hadn't eaten a good meal in awhile. It was Ray Twigg, though.

"Hello, Jake. I didn't know you came here." Jake thought Ray sounded tired.

Jake took his pop and moved down the bar to sit next to Ray. He was surprised to see him drinking so late into the night. Ray hadn't really been a heavy drinker in the army.

"You look lousy, Ray."

Ray didn't argue. "I feel lousy."

"How's the head?"

Ray's eyes flared with momentary anger. "What do you mean?"

Jake tapped the side of his own head. "Where you got hit? Does it still give you headaches?"

Jake and Ray had served together in the same company in the war. Jake had been nearby when shrapnel from a grenade had nearly ripped the side of Ray Twigg's skull off. Jake hadn't thought someone could live through that, but Ray had. He'd gone home after he had been released from the hospital. In the few times Jake had seen Raymond since the war, Jake had asked about the wound. Ray had once said that it caused him headaches.

Ray smiled and for a moment, Jake thought that he looked like a teenager again. "That's why I'm here. Sometimes when it hurts really bad, I can dull the pain with a bit of help."

"Do you need help a lot?"

Jake had noticed the broken veins in Ray's nose.

Ray chuckled. "You mean am I a sot? No. I can usually handle the pain all by myself. I only need a bit of help now and then."

The Rain Man

Jake felt compassion for his old army buddy. Ray had once shot a German who had been drawing a bead on Jake. He had seen the German soldier aiming at him and had known that he wouldn't be able to swing his rifle up to defend himself. Before the German could shoot, Ray had shot the German through the neck. Jake remembered that and appreciated the extension of life that Ray had given him. He wished he could find a way to return the favor to Ray.

"Why don't you go to the doctor and have him take a look at your head? Maybe there's still something wrong," Jake suggested.

Ray looked skeptical and rolled his eyes. "After all this time? Besides, I've been to doctors. Lots of them. None of them have helped."

"It wouldn't hurt. Maybe they can give you something better for the pain than whiskey."

"I don't want them poking and prodding my head again. I've seen doctors, lots of them. None of them did me any good. It's the rain. The pain always comes with the rain. When the rain goes, so will the pain," Raymond explained.

"They say it's going to rain for awhile. A few people are even talking about it flooding."

Ray groaned.

"I know how you feel," Jake said.

Ray snorted. "You think so?"

"Not the pain you're feeling, but I am certainly dreading any flooding as much as you are." Jake put his hand on Ray's shoulder. "Go see a doctor, Ray. I know one who can help you. Her name is Dr. Chris Evans. She's got an office on Second Street or she'll be at the hospital. Go see her. She can help you."

Ray nodded. "Maybe I will. I don't know if I can handle a full day of rain if the pain's going to be this bad."

"Why don't you do that? Tell her that I sent you, and she'll take extra good care of you."

Jake finished his pop and sighed. "That tasted good. Well, I've got to check in at the station." Jake paused. "Are you sure you're going to be all right, Ray? You don't look well at all."

Ray looked up. "All right? Probably not, but I'll get by."

"Call me if you need a ride to the doctor. Don't take any chances, you hear?"

"I'll call if I need you."

Jake nodded and left.

10

Monday, March 16, 1936
10:21 p.m.

R aymond watched Jake walk out of Johnny's Place and into the rain. It seemed to embrace him in a way it never did Raymond. To Raymond, the rain only brought pain.

He didn't mind Jake and his good intentions, but the man was a cop. Raymond couldn't take any chances around the police after what happened earlier. The police were looking for the Rain Man, but the Rain Man had found the perfect hiding place inside of Raymond.

The Rain Man laughed inside Raymond's head. Raymond winced at the deep, heaving laugh.

When Jake had gone, Raymond asked for a bottle of Old Quaker Whiskey, paid his bill and left Johnny's Place.

Outside, he hunched up his shoulders and pulled his hat down as far as he could. There was still a gap between his overcoat and hat that kept letting in rain. It ran down his neck giving him chills.

He wasn't sure how long he had been sitting inside the bar and drinking. He had come there after the Rain Man had kept him from killing himself in his room by making him pass out from pain. There had been a dozen people in the bar when he had arrived. Everyone had gradually gone home except for Johnny, old Albert and Raymond. Now Raymond seriously considered getting drunk enough to weaken the Rain Man and try to kill himself again.

The pounding of the rain on his head only aided the pain. It brought tears to his eyes.

A flood! A flood! I will be in my glory. I will be powerful! the Rain Man said.

Raymond concentrated on not screaming out loud and running in front of a truck to end his pain. He could beat this. He could. He knew he could.

And those questions Jake had been asking the bartender. The police had found the dead body and were investigating what had happened to the man. Jake knew the man came to Johnny's Place, but Raymond couldn't remember meeting him. Would Jake find all of the answers he was searching for? Raymond didn't know. He couldn't remember anything about last night.

They will get you.

"But I didn't do anything," Raymond complained.

You killed a man.

"Not me. It was you. I can't remember anything about it."

But the blood was on your hands. They will catch you and they will execute you and then your pain will be gone. But you will thank me.

"I think not."

He needed help. Raymond needed to make the pain go away so that he could think about what needed to be done.

You should have let that German kill that cop.

"No, that was before you. What I did was good," Raymond insisted.

Ah, and no act of kindness ever goes unpunished.

Raymond clutched at the bottle he had purchased and pulled it from his pocket. Then he took a deep swig and hoped that it would drive away the pain.

The ninety-proof whiskey burned going down his throat and Raymond coughed.

He needed to think straight, but that was impossible.

He would either be thinking as a drunk or thinking with pain pounding his head. How would he survive? How could he stop the Rain Man?

The Rain Man laughed. *Haven't you realized yet that you can't stop me? You are my puppet. The puppet does not control the puppeteer.*

Raymond cried again.

11

Monday, March 16, 1936
10:33 p.m.

C hris stopped putting on her raincoat and looked up at the wiry man who stood next to the admitting desk on the main floor of Memorial Hospital. His bulbous nose stood out on his face because it was so out of proportion with the rest of his body. His hair was wet and dripping. His head looked like it was flat on the left side while the right side had a normal curve. He looked exhausted.

"Can I help you?" Chris asked as she stopped walking.

"Are you Dr. Evans?" the man asked.

"Yes."

She suddenly felt awkward with this stranger. Not that she would admit it to anyone. He didn't look like he was any kind of threat. It wasn't what he said that made her uncomfortable, but the look on his face. It was empty, showing no relief, anger or amazement.

"I knew you wouldn't be at your office this late so I was hoping you would be here," the man said.

Chris nodded. "I was preparing to leave. What can I do for you?"

Chris wasn't sure if she should feel pity or fear about the man. What about him worried her? His odd appearance? She prided herself on not judging a person by his or her appearance since she had been judged wrongly so many times because she was a woman. He worried her, but she wasn't sure why.

"I hurt here." He touched the flat side of his head. "Whenever the rains come, I feel pain," the man said.

"I take it that it hurts bad enough that you didn't want to wait until tomorrow to see me at my office," Chris said.

The man smiled. "That's right. Can you help me?"

"Why did you come looking for me?"

"Jake Fairgrieve said that you could help me. He said that you were a good doctor. I need help," Raymond admitted.

"What's your name?"

"Raymond Twigg." He paused and squinted in pain.

Chris stood up and approached Raymond. "Are you hurting now?"

He nodded without saying anything. Chris took him by the arm and led him down the hall. Raymond followed like an obedient dog. Why had she ever worried about him being a danger?

Chris smiled and hoped that it reassured him things would be fine. "We'll go down to an examining room and I'll take a look at you. We'll see what we can do." They walked down empty hall. "So how well do you know Jake?" Chris asked. She hadn't ever heard Jake mention a friend named Raymond before.

"We served together in France."

"Served?"

"In the army."

Chris nodded. That explained a lot. Jake never spoke of his years fighting in Europe during the war, or if he did, he spoke in very vague terms. They were his private nightmares. Chris wondered if he had ever spoken about his experiences to Melissa.

"Are you good friends?" Chris asked.

"Not really. When we see each other in town, we'll say hello and buy each other a drink. Jake thinks I saved his life in France."

Chris tried to hide her surprise.

"Did you?" she asked.

"I guess I did, but that wasn't why I shot the German. I shot him because I was supposed to do it. He just happened to be aiming at Jake when I shot him. Anybody else would have done the same thing," Raymond explained.

He made it sound unimportant, but Chris knew that saving a life was never unimportant. It would certainly mean something to Jake. It had been his life that had been saved.

They came to the examining room. Raymond hesitated when he saw the rain beating down on the window on the other side of the room.

"Are you all right?" Chris asked.

Raymond smiled. "That's what we're here to figure out."

He sat down on the examining table.

Chris looked into Raymond's ears to see if she could see some sort of infection. She doubted it because she had watched him walking down the hallway. He hadn't shown any signs of imbalance that might indicate inner ear problems.

Then she noticed the scars on the side of his head. Hair hadn't grown there but other hair had grown over it to nearly hide them.

Chris reached up and brushed the wet brown hair out of the way. Raymond's hand shot up and grabbed her hand and pulled it away. His grip was amazingly strong.

"Does it hurt if I touch you there?" she asked.

"Yes. Anything touching my head hurts, even the rain."

"What happened to cause the scarring?"

Raymond looked away from her stare. "It's a war wound."

He was obviously as reluctant to talk about his war experiences as Jake was. If he and Jake had been affected by the war, how were they able to compartmentalize the experience? It affected them in two very different ways. Jake had embraced the military life as a police officer and Raymond had gone to pieces.

"May I look closer? I'll be as gentle as I can, but I'd like to examine your scars, especially since they are where you are indicating that you hurt the most."

Raymond sighed and nodded as Chris gently brushed his hair away from the scars, making sure not to actually touch them. They formed a web across the side of Raymond's head. She ran her hand lightly over Raymond's skull. Under the puckered, pink skin, the bone dipped and bulged at odd points where it should have been smooth. Raymond winced as her fingers explored the wounds. She was not impressed by the surgery that had been performed by Raymond's doctors.

"How were you hurt? What caused these wounds?" Chris asked.

"I was in a trench in France. I raised my head at the wrong time. A shell exploded nearby. That's all I can remember about it."

"And you weren't killed?" Chris said in amazement.

"Sometimes I wish I had been," Raymond said sadly.

"How were you treated?"

Raymond shrugged. "I don't remember. I woke up in a hospital and my head was wrapped in bandages. The doctors called me a miracle, but they didn't go into a lot of detail. They had a lot of work to do. I wasn't the only one injured in that battle. They tried to explain it to me later, but I just didn't understand."

Chris stepped back. "I'd like to have some x-rays taken of your head tomorrow to see if there is any shrapnel still remaining in your head. It could be causing your pain," Chris said.

"Could there be any left after so many years?" Raymond sounded surprised and a bit hopeful.

"It isn't going to go away unless it's taken out."

"How long will it take to find out if there's something still in there?"

"First, we have to have x-rays taken. Then a surgeon would have to determine if any shrapnel in your head could be safely removed. We'd have to schedule the surgery, which could be in the next few days and the surgery itself could take hours."

"That's tomorrow. I'm hurting now, and it's only getting worse with all the rain," Raymond nearly whined.

"I'll get you a strong painkiller that should help until we figure out what to do," Chris suggested.

Raymond sighed. "That would be good. Thank you."

"Lay down. I'll go find a nurse to go get a prescription for you. Then I'll get some x-rays taken of your head."

He obediently laid down on the table and Chris walked into the hallway. She saw Rutherford moving down the hallway toward her. He grinned and looked her up and down. She felt almost as if he could see through her clothes. Chris wanted to slap him across the face.

He stopped in front of her. "Hello, Chris. I am glad we now have an understanding."

"Oh, I understand you."

Vincent grinned and moved close enough to her that her breasts were touching his chest. He slid his hand inside her open lab coat and laid it on her hip. She closed her eyes and tried to wish him away.

"I think we'll get along just fine then," Rutherford said.

"Just leave me alone. I'm trying to do my job," Chris told him.

"No, you're trying to do a man's job. Come to my bed and I'll show you how you should be doing your job," he whispered.

He squeezed her buttock. Chris clenched her teeth to keep from slapping him. She was actually surprised to hear herself whimper.

Raymond stepped out of the examining room. He looked from Chris to Rutherford and back.

"Are you all right, Dr. Evans?" he asked.

She looked over at him and tried to blink away the tears. She didn't want anyone seeing her as weak.

"Things will be all right, Raymond," she told him.

She tried to move away, but Rutherford blocked her.

"I have to get to work," Chris said again.

"In a minute. I think you need to kiss me goodbye."

"Just because you got away with this before doesn't mean you always will," she warned him.

He grinned. "I always have."

Rutherford leaned in closer to kiss her, but Raymond grabbed him and pulled him away. Chris looked at Raymond. He had his eyes clenched shut as if he was in pain. He wasn't looking at either Chris or Rutherford.

"Leave her alone," Raymond said. Chris was surprised to hear his voice. It sounded different, more confident and deeper.

"Go back into the room, sir," Rutherford said, trying to resume his appearance as a dignified doctor.

"You were being rude to the doctor," Raymond said.

"This is none of your business."

"She is my doctor."

Rutherford sighed and then suddenly smiled at Raymond. "Sir, I wasn't being rude. You see, Chris and I besides being colleagues, are also involved romantically." His tone was friendly and man-to-man. It was a tone that was condescending to Chris even though it wasn't being directed toward her.

Raymond opened his eyes. "You are a lying bastard, and if you don't leave now, I'm going to complain about your disgraceful behavior."

Chris was surprised to hear Raymond take such a strong stand.

Vincent was, too. He backed away.

"I'm sorry you're upset, sir. I'll be leaving now and hopefully, Chris will be able to help you." As he walked by Chris, he whispered. "It's not over, Lady. We've got some things to settle between us."

Chris turned to Raymond. He had his eyes clenched shut again.

"Raymond, are you all right?" Chris touched him lightly on his head.

He shook his head. "Not yet. I'm still waiting for the medicine."

"Thank you for what you did for me," Chris said.

"He was being rude, and he's a coward. He didn't want anyone else to know what he was doing to you," Raymond said.

"But you helped me and I appreciate it."

"You're welcome."

Raymond sighed. Then he opened his eyes. "Can we get my medicine now? I don't know how much longer I can stand this."

"Why don't you come with me? I'll get you a pill right now before the pharmacist even fills the prescription."

Raymond smiled and said, "Thank you. You're an angel...a guardian angel."

12

Monday, March 16, 1936
11:00 p.m.

Chris paused at the front door to her home on Chase Street, reluctant to go inside. She was tired, but she knew she wouldn't be able to relax inside. Her work was only beginning.

She should have learned by now not to get so involved in her work. She couldn't help it, though. Chris knew her work was being watched when she was at the hospital so she had to be at her best all of the time. Concentrating on helping other people also allowed her to forget about what waited for her at home.

She stood on the porch, staring across the street. She could see her neighbors, the McAllisters, through the front window of their house. Peter and Harriet McAllister and their three children were in the living room. The children were dressed for bed and Peter was reading them a story.

Chris stopped a sigh before it escaped her by pressing her lips tightly together. When the McAllisters finished the story and bowed their heads to say an evening prayer, Chris turned away.

She opened the door to her house and went inside. The house was cold. She touched the radiator by the door. It was off. She would need to turn up the furnace to take the chill off.

She saw the curtains fluttering over a nearby window and realized that the windows were up. She shut the window and noticed the puddle of water on the hardwood oak floor.

"Dad!" she called.

There was no answer, but she could hear a record playing in another room. He must have fallen asleep listening to Benny Goodman or another of the big bands that he liked.

Chris rolled her eyes. She hurried upstairs to get a towel to sop up the water on the floors before they were ruined. She shut three more windows on the way, but only one had a puddle of water under it. Before she went downstairs, she made sure that the windows upstairs in the bedrooms were shut.

She went downstairs and threw a towel on the puddle. The yellow fabric immediately darkened as it soaked up the water. Then she opened the pocket doors and walked into the living room. Her father was sitting on the sofa reading the newspaper and listening to static on the radio.

He was a tall man who kept his hair trimmed very short. It was still black. It looked lighter, though, because his skull showed through the thin layer of hair. He had on only an undershirt and acted as if the room was warm.

"Didn't you hear me call you?" Chris asked.

Her father looked up and she noticed he wasn't wearing his glasses once again. He was squinting at the newspaper. Chris shook her head and sighed.

"I did hear you, and I thought that it was quite unbecoming for a lady to be yelling in the house," he said in a scolding tone.

"It's my house. I can do as I want," Chris snapped.

"That's being very petulant, dear."

He laid aside the newspaper and stood up to give her a hug and a kiss on the cheek. His hands felt like bones when he laid them on her shoulders.

"It's good you're home," he said. "I'm hungry."

Which meant, in her father's language, "When are you going to cook me dinner?"

"You could have made yourself a sandwich," Chris said.

"You know I can't cook."

"That's not cooking! Even I could do it."

Chris couldn't cook very well, and she really didn't feel like attempting to cook something this late. To her, cooking was as foreign as medicine was to many of the patients she treated. It was a chore that she hated along with all of the other housekeeping chores that her father refused to do because he considered it "woman's work."

Chris stepped back from her father and reminded herself not to yell at him. It never accomplished anything and Chris always wound up feeling guilty afterwards.

She walked into the kitchen and began to make peanut butter and jelly sandwiches and canned soup. Those were two items that she thought she could handle. She certainly wasn't going to go back out in the rain to get something at a restaurant, which is what she did when she got tired of her meager cooking skills.

As she made the meal, Chris wondered if this is what it would be like being married to Jake. Would he expect her to wait on him hand and foot like her father? Would he want her to stay home and have kids? Would they sit down every night to a nice meal like the McAllisters did?

"I'm hungry, Christine!" her father called.

Chris rolled her eyes and swallowed her harsh reply.

She reminded herself that her father hadn't always been like this. When her mother had been alive, her father had run a small grocery store in Catonsville. Her mother had cooked and cleaned and kept house like so many other women, but Chris's father hadn't depended on his wife like he depended on Chris now. He just hadn't been the same since her mother had died from consumption. Grief had driven him to incapacity.

Chris laid the top slice of bread on the sandwiches and then poured the hot soup into bowls. She set the meal on a tray and carried it out to the dining room. Her father was already seated at the table. She put his soup and sandwich in front of him.

He looked at the meal, but he didn't say anything. They had come to a truce about that issue at least. He had complained one time about the quality of a meal Chris had made for him. Chris had been particularly tired that night so she had simply dumped his meal in the garbage and gone to bed. Her father hadn't complained anymore after that.

They ate in silence. Her father didn't make conversation any longer. Chris remembered how he used to tell stories about the people who had come into the store and the news of the day. He used to be able to offer wonderful insights on government and society using the real examples of people in the neighborhood. Mr. Nelson the postman was an example of perseverance. Mrs. Johnston and her children portrayed the problem of the growth of government. Now he just didn't seem to care.

What if Chris did marry Jake, not that he would have her? What would they do about her father? He and Jake had never met. How would Jake react to him?

Since her father stayed inside the house not even venturing onto the porch, no one knew him. If they did, she was sure the stories would have circulated through town about the woman doctor's crazy father.

The Rain Man

One of the reasons that Chris had moved here was because her father had always spoken lovingly of the mountains, but now he wouldn't even sit on the porch on warm afternoons. She wasn't even sure if he looked out the windows to know where he was.

She didn't mind living in Cumberland. Not really.

What she did mind was that she had become a mother before she became a wife.

"It's getting close to twelve o'clock, dad," Chris said as they finished dinner.

He looked up, surprised. "It can't be noon."

Chris closed her eyes and took a deep breath. It wasn't that her father was losing his mind. He just didn't care about things anymore to the point where he didn't even pay attention to little things like what the time of day was.

"It's not noon. It's midnight. Look outside," Chris said.

Her father glanced over his shoulder to look out the window. He saw that it was dark outside and frowned.

"Oh, I guess that's why I was finding it hard to read the blasted newspaper." He shook the folded copy of the *Cumberland Evening Times* angrily.

"Or it could be that you're not wearing your glasses."

"Don't get sassy, young lady."

Chris bit her lips shut to keep from saying something she would regret. She hated when her father tried to treat her like she was ten years old.

"If you haven't noticed, Dad, I'm no longer a young woman."

"Of course you are. You're just barely thirty. That's still young. If you feel old, it's because you look behind you and see nothing there to mark that you've been on this earth."

Or maybe it's because I have to take care of a man who doesn't care if he lives, Chris thought.

"What do you see behind you?" Chris asked.

"I see you. I know I continued my line and I know that if you are alive so is a piece of your mother. I see you and I see a younger her. That makes me feel young. That makes me feel satisfied."

Chris sighed. She just couldn't stay mad at her father. He might be hard to get along with, but she knew that he loved her.

"It's time for bed, Dad," she said.

"Of course it is. It's dark out."

He stood up. He wiped his mouth with the linen napkin and laid it on the table. Chris started to follow him up the stairs, but he shooed her away.

"I can tuck myself in quite well, Christine," her father told her.

Sometimes she doubted that. Still, she knew it would do no good to argue with him. She did stay at the bottom of the stairs to watch him and make sure that he went into his room.

She walked out onto her front porch. Across the street, the McAllisters had gone to bed and their house was dark. The rain still came down steadily. She sat on the porch swing and watched it come down.

Chris had never been in Cumberland during a flood, but she had heard stories of the 1924 floods. None of them had come from Jake, though. He wouldn't talk about flooding. On the other hand, Veronica, her nurse receptionist, seemed fascinated by the subject. She talked about the possibility of another flood whenever it rained, even if it was only a light shower.

Chris just couldn't imagine Cumberland flooding. Not only would the rivers have to rise substantially, but she couldn't understand how the rivers could continue to rise over their banks once they had plenty of room to spread out.

It was rain. Heavy rain, granted, but just rain.

Chris stood up and walked to the porch railing. She watched a small wave of dark water roll down the hill toward Fayette Street. It was only an inch deep, but it spread from curb to curb.

There was also water rushing down Fayette Street, but she wasn't sure how deep that was. She couldn't tell from this distance. All that water would eventually run into the sewers and Wills Creek.

Chris watched the water for a few moments more. She could understand how flooding could come to Cumberland.

She shivered.

13

Tuesday, March 17, 1936
2:51 p.m.

Raymond rolled onto his stomach and pulled his pillow over his head. He wanted to stop the sound of the rain drumming against his window. Each raindrop striking the window sounded like a finger tapping the side of his skull. One by itself did not hurt, but each one hitting together and quickly made Raymond feel like he was being punched in the side of the head.

He groaned and sat up in the bed. The room was dark, but he could see the outlines of the window against the night sky and the rain splashing against the panes.

He walked across the room and took a pair of the pain pills that Dr. Evans had given him. He only had two more left, though she had said there were enough pills to last for at least two days. She'd been wrong. Here it was not even a night gone by and Raymond was nearly out of pills. He'd been taking them every hour instead of every four hours.

He would have to get more tomorrow. What would Dr. Evans say when he came into her office asking for more pills? The pills hadn't helped much. They seemed to bring relief for only a few minutes. After that, the insistent rain worked itself back into his head and made him hurt again.

His real hope lay with what Dr. Evans had told him about his injury. He could be healed by surgery. He could banish the Rain Man forever.

Inside his head, the Rain Man laughed hard. Raymond held his hands over his ears as if to keep out the sound of the laughter, but he couldn't keep out something that was already in his head.

I can ease your pain. Let me help, the Rain Man urged.

Raymond shook his head. He had an idea of what the Rain Man's help would be. He didn't want anything to do with it...but the pain! His head was on fire! Why weren't the pills working?

No pill can erase me, Raymond. Only I can ease the pain.

"No, the pills will stop the pain. They worked earlier. Dr. Evans promised me they would work," Raymond muttered.

No pill can stop this pain. The doctor lied. She wants to trap you. They know you have power and they want to steal it. No one understands you like I do. Let me ease your pain.

Streaks of sharp, stabbing sensations slid over his head. Raymond whimpered and slipped off the bed onto his knees on the floor.

"Oh, God!" he muttered.

The Rain Main laughed. *Yes, now you begin to understand. I am your god! I can exalt you or destroy you!*

Raymond's eyes rolled up into his head as the pressure on his skull increased. He collapsed onto the floor.

Rain hit Raymond in the face. Had the windows finally broken under the constant pounding of the rain? No. He was standing on a street someplace unfamiliar. He wasn't sure if he was even still in Cumberland, but he assumed that he was. He hoped that he was.

He stood under a tree. He wasn't wearing his raincoat or hat. The tree didn't give him much protection, either. It hadn't bloomed leaves yet so the rain fell between the branches and hit him on the head.

He was staring at an unfamiliar brick house. It looked fairly large with a wide porch around two sides and a side yard. Raymond blinked and wiped the rain from his eyes.

The pain in his head had receded somewhat, but he still hurt. Raymond turned around to leave. He'd find a street sign and figure out where he was.

Don't go, the Rain Man said.

"I don't like the rain. I want to get indoors," Raymond said.

Then the pain will return. I can help you.

"Why here?"

Here is where we can end the pain if you wait.

Raymond didn't mind waiting, not if it meant ending the pain. It was better than the alternative where the Rain Man was concerned. He huddled close to the trunk of the maple tree, hoping to find at least a small amount of shelter from the falling rain.

"I should take another pill."

No, you don't need the doctor's pills. What you need is me. I can free you from the pain for longer than the pill. Trust me.

The Rain Man

Raymond couldn't. He knew what the Rain Man could do if he was trusted totally.

About twenty minutes later, a man stepped out onto the porch of the house across the street. The man was in the shadows so Raymond couldn't see his face. All he could see was the glowing end of the cigarette the man was smoking.

The Rain Man chuckled and Raymond felt his body tense. This was whom he had been waiting for.

"Who is he?" Raymond asked.

He is the end of the pain.

Raymond wasn't sure what the Rain Man meant, but the tone of the voice in his head scared him. Then again, it always scared him.

"I'm leaving," Raymond said.

No. Not yet.

The man on the porch raised his umbrella and stepped off the porch. Raymond wished that he had an umbrella. The man started up the street toward his car. Surprisingly, Raymond felt himself following. He was no longer in control. The Rain Man was.

As the man climbed into his Ford coupe, Raymond walked up beside the open door. The man fumbled to lower his umbrella. Raymond hefted a rock that he hadn't realized was in his hand.

The man looked up at Raymond. "You!"

"Take me to where the flooding will begin," Raymond said.

"What are you talking about?"

"North," Raymond said, "I want to be where the flooding is beginning." He tapped the side of his head. "I can feel it here. It has begun."

The man frowned and shook his head. "You're crazy."

Raymond frowned. "You shouldn't have said that."

He smashed the rock into the man's head and he fell back into the car. Raymond pushed him to the passenger side of the car. The key was already in the ignition. Raymond started the car and drove away.

Raymond wasn't sure where he was driving. He kept glancing over at the man. He did recognize him, but Raymond wasn't sure where he recognized him from.

He drove into North End and through the Narrows, following Wills Creek and stopping occasionally to stare at the dark water. The river surged through the channel threatening to breach its banks at many points. Raymond found a spot where the creek was overflowing its banks and he parked the car.

When he dragged the man out of the passenger side, Raymond finally recognized him. It was the doctor from Memorial Hospital who had been bothering Dr. Evans.

It took you long enough. He'll take the pain with him and you'll do that woman a favor.

"How?" Raymond asked.

Raymond picked the rock up from inside of the car and smashed the man on the left side of the head again. Blood flowed freely from a scalp wound.

Harder! the Rain Man urged.

Raymond hit the doctor again and again until he finally heard the skull crack. Raymond finally stopped. His hands were drenched in blood. He threw the rock into the creek.

Now the body.

Raymond tumbled the body into the fast-flowing water. The pain was fading, but in its place was the guilt that Raymond had killed another man, even a bad person like Dr. Rutherford. He began to cry as he looked at the body floating face down in the water.

Raymond held his hands up into the sky, acknowledging the power of the falling rain. Then he laughed.

Raymond blinked away the rain in his eyes as he regained control of his body. He caught sight of the body in the water and realized what had happened.

"Not again!" he wept.

It was too soon. The rain was too powerful. The pain was too great.

Raymond cried as he drove back through town and parked the car in an empty parking lot near a church on Oldtown Road. He walked from there back to his room.

At his room, he pulled off his wet, blood-stained clothes and threw them into the basin on the nightstand and tried to rinse the blood from them. Then he hung them over the radiator to dry.

Raymond stared out the window and saw the raindrops running down the panes. Each drop of rain meant pain for him. Then he noticed the pill bottle on the sill. He considered taking another pill, but realized he didn't hurt.

Raymond smiled. He climbed into his bed and fell fast asleep.

14

Tuesday, March 17, 1936
8:05 a.m.

Jake arranged the papers on his desk as he did every morning before he left. While his desk might be messy as he processed cases and sorted through notes, he always left it neat and organized. It made it easier for him to get started working at the beginning of his next shift.

He didn't feel relieved to be heading home. He'd spent the night tracking down other railroaders who might have seen Mark Connelly at Johnny's Place last night. Jake had talked to six sleepy men during the night and none of them had given him any useful information. Mark Connelly had been alive when they had all seen him last.

Lieutenant Lewellen stopped by Jake's desk on his way home. He had his raincoat and hat on, ready to leave himself.

"Don't look so glum, Jake," he said.

"I feel like I missed something about that murder case. It's been bugging me all night, but I can't seem to make whatever connection it is that my mind seems to want to make," Jake replied.

Lewellen frowned and lit a cigarette. "Maybe that's because there is no connection; no connection between the murderer and the victim, no connection between the victim and the location and no motive for the murder."

Jake shook his head and rubbed his tired eyes. "I just don't know. There's something I'm not understanding."

"Whoever really understands a murderer? You did everything you could, Jake. You canvassed the area. You talked to friends and family and visited the home and workplace. I don't see what else you could do. I think your initial theory that the murderer was a hobo that Connelly caught doing something he shouldn't is the most-likely answer," Lewellen told him.

"Most likely maybe, but not one that I can prove." Besides, Jake still thought that if the murderer had been a hobo, the murder would have happened much closer to the rail yard.

"Well, you can't do anything about it right now. Go home, Jake, and sleep on it. Things will look better in the afternoon. The rain may have even stopped."

Lewellen left and Jake stood up. The day shift was at work and there was no reason to stay. He waved to a few of the other officers as he walked over to the coat rack to put on his coat. The rain might be ended by afternoon, but for now, it was still coming down steadily.

It would be a wet city election this morning.

He walked down Mechanic Street to Market Street and crossed the bridge over Wills Creek. The water was definitely rising now. Jake couldn't deny it no matter how much he might like to. There was going to be flooding of some sort in the city.

The sight of the dark water surging through the creek channel scared Jake. It reminded him too much of the 1924 flood that had killed Mel. He and Melissa had been visiting friends the night of the flood. On their way home, their car had gotten mired in mud. Jake and Melissa had climbed out of the car to walk home. The flood current had been too strong, though, and it had swept them into the Potomac. Jake had been so frantic to try and stay afloat that he hadn't been any help to Mel. When he had finally been able to grab onto a log floating down the river, he had looked around for Melissa, but she was gone. Searchers had found her body among a pile of debris after the flood waters had receded.

That had happened almost twelve years ago. Jake had been a widower more than twice as long as he had been married, but it still seemed like Melissa had been killed yesterday.

As he neared his home, Jake saw lights on on the first floor. If it hadn't been raining, Jake would have been tempted to stay outside. He really wasn't in the mood for company this morning.

He stepped onto the porch and shook as much water off himself as he could. He might be willing to puddle the floor at Henny's Restaurant, but he didn't want to bring it into his own home.

He stepped inside and smelled bacon cooking. That brought a smile to his face.

"I figured that would warm you up before you start complaining," his sister said.

Virginia stepped from the dining room into the living room. She was an attractive blond who had a radiant smile. She was casually dressed in a pink blouse and red skirt.

A little girl who looked just like Virginia peeked out from between Virginia's legs.

"Hi, Uncle Jake," the five-year-old said.

"Hello, Jessica," Jake said to his niece.

Then he glared at his sister.

Virginia chuckled. "Don't give me that look. It hasn't worked yet. It doesn't even work with Jessica anymore. What makes you think it will start working now?"

Jake rolled his eyes. He knew better than to argue. He had family members visiting his house at least three days a week. It wasn't always his sister who came to see him. It could just as easily be his aunts, uncles, cousins or mother. His sister came the most frequently, though.

"Well, if you have to be here at least you brought food," Jake said with a grumpiness he didn't feel. He was, however, tired.

"I helped Mama make the eggs," Jessica said.

"Then I know it will taste good. Your mother can't cook, but I know you can." He ruffled her hair.

Jessica smiled. Virginia waved a wooden spoon in his direction.

"Watch out, big brother, or that breakfast will wind up on your lap. Now go wash up. You, too, Jessica," Virginia said.

Jake turned away. Since Mel's death, his family had refused to let him slip into depression. They kept him company even when he didn't want it. They brought him meals and ate with him. At first, it had been necessary to keep Jake from going crazy with grief, but now his family did it from habit.

His was a close family that had lived in Cumberland for over a century. Jake's father had died young from black lung disease because of his work in the Eckhart Mines, but that hadn't diminished the size of his family.

"So where's Phil?" Jake asked. Phillip Hendrickson was Virginia's husband.

"He got called in to help out at the fire station today in case there is flooding," Virginia told him.

"So what brought you out in this rain?" Jake asked his sister as he sat down at the dining room table.

"I was worried that all this rain would cause some flooding, and I knew that would worry you. The creek looked high when we drove over the bridge," she said quietly.

"So you came to hold my hand?"

Virginia shook her head. "No, I came to feed you breakfast."

Jake smiled.

Virginia set a plate filled with fried eggs, bacon and home fries in front of him. Then she uncovered a basket of fresh-baked biscuits. The three of them sat down at the kitchen table and ate. Jessica chattered incessantly about the rain and how it kept her from playing outside. Jake just tried to ignore the rain.

When the meal was finished, Jake helped his sister clear the table and wash the dishes. Then Virginia bundled Jessica up in her coat and hat and put on her own.

Jake was surprised to feel a sense of loss as they prepared to leave. He didn't want to be alone today. It was almost as if he was a child afraid of the dark, but it was the rain that he feared and his family was the light to keep him calm.

Jessica hugged him goodbye.

"Stay dry, Squirt," he told her.

Virginia kissed him on the cheek. "Take care of yourself, Big Brother. The rain will stop. It always does."

"I know. I'm just worried about when it will stop," Jake told her.

15

Tuesday, March 17, 1936
1:03 p.m.

Jake woke up and rolled over to look at the clock on the night stand. He'd only been in bed for a little over four hours. Why had he awakened? He usually slept to about six o'clock when he was working night shift.

Then he heard the telephone ringing downstairs. That must have been what had awakened him. He didn't rush to get it because anyone who knew him wouldn't be calling him now. Someone really wanted to talk to him. The phone rang for least a dozen times. He was tempted to get up and answer it.

Finally, it stopped and he lay in bed dreading the day ahead. He was worried, but he couldn't understand why or about what. He just felt a sense of foreboding. He could still hear the rain coming down outside.

He climbed out of bed and walked over to the bedroom window. Outside, small rivers ran down the side of the road next to the curb. How far behind was the flooding? That rain was a bad sign.

Was it really the rain that was upsetting him or his dream?

Jake had dreamed that the dead man he had seen in the alley yesterday was actually Raymond Twigg. Jake supposed it could just be a random dream connecting two events from yesterday, but it somehow seemed correct. It wasn't that Ray had been killed, but there was something familiar about the dead man. Something had struck a cord with Jake, though he couldn't say why.

Since he and Ray had served in the same company during the war, Jake wondered if Mark Connelly had been someone that he also knew from the war. If he was, Jake couldn't place him in his memories either by face or by name.

No, Jake was sure that he didn't know Mark Connelly. So what was so familiar about the man? Had it been his clothes? Jake thought about that. It was possible. Jake knew many railroaders and Connelly had been dressed like many of them in overalls and a flannel shirt.

While Jake considered it, it still didn't seem right and it wouldn't explain why he had thought about Ray being the dead man.

Jake showered. He wondered why he even bothered since he was sure he would be soaked to the skin by the time he finished work this evening. Why get himself wet on purpose?

The phone began ringing again. Since Jake was already awake, he answered it. It was Bud Seeler, the desk sergeant.

"Good, I finally got a hold of you," Bud said.

"Finally? Was that you who called earlier?" Jake asked.

"Yes, and you didn't answer."

"That's because I was asleep."

"Well, you need to come into work."

Jake rubbed his forehead with his free hand. "I will in about seven hours."

"Not then. Now. We've got trouble."

"What sort of trouble?" he said, suspecting what the problem was.

"The river is rising, and it looks like it will flood. We need all hands out to move stuff here so we'll be ready to help out when the water comes. Why do you think I'm here this early? We're going to be busy all day and night."

Jake groaned and shook his head. "I'm getting dressed now. Let me eat and then I'll come in."

He hung up the phone and finished dressing. Then he headed out to Henny's Restaurant for supper.

Jake noticed that although the water was running down the street, the sewers seemed to still be keeping up with the demand. How much longer that would last though was hard to say.

As he crossed the Baltimore Street Bridge, Jake noticed that the water was noticeably higher. In fact, it was uncomfortably high. Jake admitted to himself that it would flood. He only hoped that it wouldn't be a bad one.

While he was waiting to cross Mechanic Street and the intersection with Baltimore, he looked in the window of Metro Clothes and saw the employees packing up their stock. Joe Feldstein and his employees were taking precautions.

Jake entered the restaurant ready to yell at Art if he made a comment about Jake bringing in the rain with him. Flooding put both of them in a foul mood.

He was surprised when he saw a woman behind the counter cooking hamburger on the stove. She was a middle-aged woman with brown hair that was tied up in a bun on the back of her head.

"Who are you?" Jake asked.

"Ruth. I'm Art's wife," the woman said. Her voice was much higher pitched than Jake would have expected.

"What happened to Art? I've never known him to miss work," Jake asked as he sat down with Harvey McIntyre. Bill was undoubtedly at work and Jake was surprised to find Harvey here.

"He couldn't get out of bed today," Ruth said.

"Is he sick?"

Ruth shook his head. "No, it's his knee. Rain always causes it to hurt, but it was so bad this morning that he couldn't even put any weight on it. He tried to get out of bed and as soon as he stood up, he fell right back down." Ruth paused. "Are you Jake?"

Jake nodded.

"Art said to tell you 'I told you so.'"

Harvey laughed, "Even when he's not here, Art still manages to give you grief, Jake."

They all laughed, but Jake was still concerned. Jake understood what Art was trying to tell him. Art's psychic knee had been right. This was going to be a gullywasher of a storm and there would be flooding in town.

"Did Art also tell you what I like to eat?" Jake asked.

Ruth nodded. "He did. I got it started when I figured you were Jake. It will be ready in a bit."

Jake certainly couldn't complain about the service when Art was sick.

"So are you watching the polls today, Jake?" Harvey asked.

"No. I got called in early. They're expecting flooding sometime today. I doubt many people will be showing up to vote with the weather this bad. They will have bigger things on their mind like whether their house will still be in Cumberland tomorrow," Jake replied.

"I wonder if a house floats out of the city limits if the person who lives there is still considered a city resident and can vote," Harvey joked.

"That depends on whether they vote before their house floats away or after," Jake said.

"So you think the flooding will be that bad?"

Jake pointed to Ruth. "Art's not here, is he? When was the last time that happened?"

"I see in the newspaper that you were busy yesterday." Harvey turned the morning edition of the *Cumberland Daily News* around and pointed to the article. The headline read: "South End Man Murdered in Alley."

"Did you know Mark Connelly?" Jake asked. Harvey lived in South End on Louisiana Avenue.

Harvey shook his head. "Nope. I know an Andrew Connelly, but that man's old enough to be this one's father."

"Too bad. I could use a break on that case. Mark Connelly was just an average Joe."

Harvey frowned. "So don't you think you will catch the murderer?"

Jake shrugged. "I sure as hell want to, but no one seemed to see anything. I'd hate to think that someone who could kill a man in the way Mark Connelly was killed could still be walking around to do it again."

"So it was messy, huh?"

"I haven't seen a death that messy since the war," Jake said. "I…"

Jake stopped. He suddenly realized what his dream had been trying to tell him. It wasn't that he had seen Ray Twigg as the dead man. The connection was that Jake had seen Ray after he had been wounded in France. The same side of his head had been crushed as Mark Connelly's. As Ray had lain on the ground being treated by the medic, he had looked like Mark Connelly. They had the same type of wound on the same side of the head.

That is what made Jake connect the dead man and Ray.

Still, was it anything more than a coincidence? Would he have made the connection if he hadn't seen Ray in the bar?

But Jake had seen Ray in the bar that Connelly had frequented. Was that a coincidence, too?

Ray had talked about the pain from his wound and easing the pain. How did he go about doing that? Drown himself in booze? That was what he implied.

Jake quickly ate his meal when Ruth set it in front of him. He didn't know when he would have a chance to eat again if the city flooded later today.

"Slow down boy," Harvey said. "You've still got time. Just tell Chief Eyerman that the rain slowed you down. No one's going to be rushing out to vote in weather like this."

"It's not that. I've got to check something out before they send me to the polls," Jake said between bites of ham.

He finished off the last of his coffee and dropped three dimes and a nickel on the table. Then he put on his hat and raincoat. He headed out the door, waving to everyone as he left.

"Hey, Jake!" Harvey called as Jake reached the door.

Jake turned around. "What?"

"Happy St. Patrick's Day!"

Jake rolled his eyes and left.

When he got to City Hall, he went in the entrance to the police department. He paused only to stare at the puddle of water forming on the floor. It had spread across most of the floor since last night.

"Not good news, is it?" Bud said as he walked by.

Jake shook his head. "I hadn't thought about headquarters flooding."

"Right now, that's about all I can think of. We're going to start moving things upstairs now because if the water gets any higher in here that means we'll be busy in town and won't have the opportunity to move it then," the desk sergeant explained.

Jake looked at the growing puddle again and shook his head.

It's going to flood again like in my nightmares, he thought.

"Are the files still down here?" Jake asked, trying to focus on his job at hand.

Bud nodded. "Most of them."

Jake hung his rain slicker up and headed for the file room. The room was about fifteen by fifteen feet square. File cabinets ran around the sides and there were also a few in the center of the room. Jake started looking on the tags on each drawer until he found the one for "Tu-Tz."

Jake pulled open the drawer and found a file folder for "Twigg, Raymond Charles." He hadn't been sure that there would be a file. Jake still remembered Ray as a quiet young soldier who rarely even drank. Since he had no hesitations about drinking any longer, it shouldn't be surprising that he had a police record. Even likable Mark Connelly had had a record.

Jake carried the file back out to his desk and sat down. He opened the folder and began to leaf through the documents.

The first thing Jake saw was a report on a fight that Ray had been in right before Christmas 1935. It had happened outside of Johnny's Place. Ray and a man named Spencer O'Rourke had gotten into an argument in the street and started fighting. It was a typical drunken brawl. The report said that when police arrived Ray had been repeatedly punching O'Rourke on the left side of his head.

Another fight took place in a bar seven months before the Christmas fight. That fight had been in a bar in South Cumberland called End of the Tracks. Ray had been slamming a man's head against the bar when police arrived. The victim had suffered a concussion.

Other incidents showed that Ray had over a dozen arrests and all of them for fighting. Jake also noticed that in all of them, Ray had been attacking the other man's head and when a side of the head was noted, it was the left side.

Just like Mark Connelly.

Jake shivered.

Besides slamming heads against a building or bars, Ray had attacked men with stones and bottles. In one of the earlier incidents, Ray had even tried to crush a man's head in his hands. In that incident, Ray had complained about the pain in his head and told police, "The Rain Man told me to do it! He told me. I didn't want to, but the Rain Man said it would stop the pain." The officer who had written the report had originally written "Raymond" instead of "Rain Man," then changed it. Jake thought about that for awhile, but he wasn't sure what Raymond had been talking about no matter which way Raymond had said it. Neither had the police. Could Raymond have been talking about himself? Ray had refused to explain who the Rain Man was.

Jake did understand about Ray's pain. Ray had been feeling pain from his wounds even back then. It was that pain that drove him to drink. Did Ray suffer a severe personality change when he drank? How violent could Ray get?

It was time for Jake to go back to Johnny's Place.

16

Tuesday, March 17, 1936
1:22 p.m.

Raymond woke with pain spiking through his head. The Rain Man's relief had been shorter than usual.

Looking at the rain outside still worried him, but at the same time, he could see the bottle of pills on the sill and receive some comfort knowing they were there to help him.

Raymond opened his closet and took out a fresh white shirt. As he reached into the closet, he looked down at the bottom of the closet.

"He said I was crazy, too. I'm not. You're both wrong. He wouldn't listen to me either. At least now you listen to me when I need to talk."

Raymond quickly closed the door and put on the shirt. His suit had dried on the radiator. He put that on as well. Then he shaved using water in the pitcher heated over his camp stove. That way, he didn't have to worry about fighting for a sink in the common bathroom. He carefully combed his hair and scrubbed his face. He wished that he could wash away the dark circles under his eyes. He was still tired, though he suspected that he had slept well last night.

Raymond slipped a couple painkillers into his shirt pocket in case he needed them later.

It was hard to imagine Dr. Evans as Jake Fairgrieve's girl. It was hard to imagine her as anyone's girl. She was pretty, but he thought she acted too much like a man. She was also very different from Jake's first wife. Raymond had grown up in the same neighborhood with Melissa Pittman, and she had been a lady in the best sense of the word.

Raymond smiled. The interesting thing was that he liked both women. Maybe he and Jake were more alike than not. If so, he felt sorry for Jake.

A stab of pain lanced through his head. *Alike? You are the prey and Jake is the hunter*, the Rain Man told him.

Raymond rubbed his temples and quickly swallowed a pill.

He hoped that the painkillers would prove to be a way for him to control the Rain Man. The Rain Man had been with him for so long and Raymond had tried so many things before, he wondered if he could ever be normal. Those memories from before the war seemed so precious to him now. Those were the memories when he had been Raymond Twigg and only Raymond Twigg.

He remembered the first time that he had realized that the Rain Man was him. He had still been in the army hospital recovering from his head wounds. The pain had started at the now-familiar point on the side of his head. Then it had begun to rain outside.

It was dark outside and there was no doctor or nurse in the ward, just beds of sleeping men. Raymond lay in bed wide awake. The pain in his head made sure of that.

The soldier in the bed next to him was also awake. He was propped up on his elbows watching the rain strike the window and smiling. The pain in Raymond's head increased. It felt like his skull wanted to bust free from the bandages that held it together. He hated the man's smile. How could that man be enjoying the rain when it was bringing such pain to Raymond?

Stop him from smiling and it will ease your pain.

Raymond was surprised to hear the voice in his head, but it made sense. The other patient was enjoying the rain, but it was the rain that brought Raymond pain. If he could stop the enjoyment, he could stop the pain.

"Isn't it lovely?" the soldier asked.

"Lovely? It's making mud," Raymond said.

Kill him.

The soldier turned to him and said, "It's cleansing everything. Haven't you ever noticed the way the rain washes the smell of gunpowder from the battlefield? It's God telling us we have a chance at a fresh start if we're smart enough to take the chance."

The soldier was a boy, just as young as Raymond, but he seemed so much more innocent.

Kill him. Kill him, the voice screamed in his head.

Raymond squeezed his eyes shut and put his hands over his ears. It didn't stop him from hearing the voice.

Kill him and the pain will stop.

Raymond stood up and smacked the man in the side of the head with the metal bedpan. It made the bedpan ring with a dull gong. He hit the man right where Raymond felt his pain growing from. The man fell onto his side, halfway out of the bed.

"How does that feel?" Raymond whispered to the unconscious man. "Now you know what the rain feels like."

Raymond was rewarded with a slight lessening of his own pain. He had traded places with the man. He had taken the man's pleasure and made it his own. Raymond was smiling while the soldier was in pain. Raymond grinned and hit the man again. Then he had traded bedpans with the man and climbed back in his bed and went to sleep.

The pain was gone.

How easy it had been back then to please the Rain Man! Now it took so much more to ease the pain. The Rain Man was a greedy master. When would it become too much?

Raymond lifted the bottle of pills that Dr. Evans had given him. Maybe this time they would work. So far he felt good.

Smiling, he was almost happy, though wet, when he arrived at Wolford's Funeral Home. Of course, it wouldn't do to be too happy. It was a funeral parlor after all.

Daniel Wolford stood in the entryway to the old house when Raymond came inside.

"We have a body to prepare. He came in from the hospital this morning. He's already been embalmed, but he needs to be cleaned up and dressed," Wolford told him.

"When is the viewing?"

"This evening."

That was soon. No wonder Daniel was in such a rush.

"I recommended a closed coffin. There are just some wounds you can't do much about, but the wife insisted on an open casket."

Daniel shook his head in disbelief.

"I'll get right on it, sir."

"Good, Raymond. I knew I could count on you." Wolford patted Raymond on the shoulder.

The embalming and preparation area was in the basement of the house. The viewing rooms and office were on the first floor and Wolford had his rooms on the second floor and the attic.

Raymond turned on the lights and went downstairs. The basement smelled of formaldehyde and other chemicals, which was to be expected. Raymond had worked here for six years ever since he had lost his job with the Kelly-Springfield Tire Company. Today, though, the basement also smelled musty from the continuing rains.

He walked across the cement floor to the table at the west side of the house. The dead man had a sheet draped over his body. A suit hung from an overhead bar. This would be the suit the man would be buried in. If a body wasn't too stiff, Raymond would actually put the clothes on the person, dressing them as he would a child. If the dead person's limbs were stiff, Raymond would cut the suits and dresses down the back and pulled them onto the body and then pin the outfits closed. No one ever knew the difference, except for the dead and they didn't complain.

Raymond drew the sheet back and saw the dead man. It was a face that he had seen last night when the dead man he had been lying in the same position on the red bricks of an alleyway.

Raymond screamed.

He backed away from the body. This couldn't be happening! He had killed that man. How had they connected Raymond to the dead man? This was a set up!

He tried to calm himself, but he couldn't breathe normally. His head throbbed painfully.

"Raymond, are you all right?" Wolford asked from upstairs.

Raymond grabbed hold of the railing and swung himself around onto the steps. He bounded up the staircase, taking three steps at a time. At the top of the stairs, he plowed into Wolford without even slowing. His boss fell onto the hardwood floor as Raymond ran by him.

Then Raymond was through the front door and running into the rain, screaming as the pain in his head made him feel like it would burst.

17

Tuesday, March 17, 1936
2:14 p.m.

Jake drove to South Cumberland and parked the patrol car near Johnny's Place, which also happened to be close to the most-recent address Jake had found in the files for Ray.

He climbed out and walked up the stairs and into the lobby of the B&O Railroad YMCA. The radio in the corner broadcast the news from WTBO, and two men sat at a table near the radio playing chess. A young man with short jet-black hair sat behind the counter reading a magazine. Behind him were the rows of mail slots for the men who lived at the YMCA.

"I'm looking for Ray Twigg," Jake said.

The young man looked up and noticed Jake's uniform. "Is Raymond in trouble?"

"Not necessarily. I need to talk to him about a couple things."

The young man looked skeptical. "He's in room 403 on the top floor."

"Thanks."

Jake headed up the stairs. He considered what he would say to Ray. This was going to be uncomfortable. Ray had saved his life in the war. He wasn't a killer. What would he say to Ray without offending him?

Jake stopped in front of the scarred wooden door and knocked. He waited until he heard movement inside the room. He knocked again.

The door opened and Jake saw his former army comrade. Ray's eyes were bloodshot. He looked tired and was wearing a tattered robe.

"Hi, Ray. Did I wake you?" Jake asked as he smiled.

"I was up." His voice was flat and lifeless.

Jake could see that Ray was wearing pants underneath his robe.

"You don't look too good. Are you all right?" Jake asked.

"My head is hurting. The rain makes it worse." Ray raised his hand and rubbed his left temple.

"Can I come in?"

Ray hesitated and stepped back. "I guess."

Jake walked into the room. He sat down in the wooden chair in front of the desk. He noticed the exposed plaster lathe in the wall near the window. The room needed some repairs.

"What happened to your wall, Ray?" Jake asked.

Ray turned around and looked where Jake was staring. He shook his head and shrugged.

"The plaster gave way. I had my class picture hanging there."

Jake looked at the hole and saw that the wooden lathe strips were broken as well as plaster. A picture hadn't done that.

"What are you doing here, Jake?" Ray asked.

Ray took his sports coat off the radiator. He took off his robe and put on the sports coat.

"I wanted to talk to you about the murder case I'm working on."

Ray stopped moving with only one arm in the jacket. "Murder case? What murder case? I'm no detective."

"Remember when I saw you in Johnny's Place last night?"

Ray rubbed his temple again. "Vaguely. If you saw me in Johnny's Place, then you know what I was doing there. I'd be very lucky if I can remember being there, let alone meeting you."

"I'm trying to find information about a man named Mark Connelly. He was murdered last night, and he used to spend a lot of time in Johnny's Place. He was there yesterday evening before he was killed. I'm trying to find out if anyone saw him leave with someone."

"So why do you want to talk to me about it?"

Now was the moment of truth. How would Jake handle this?

"I started thinking about how the man was killed. It reminded me of your wounds from the war," Jake said slowly.

Ray self-consciously touched the side of his head where it was misshapen. Jake wondered if the man realized that he was touching the wound. "So? He wasn't killed by shrapnel, was he?"

Jake shook his head. "No. His head was crushed against the street, but the wound was on the same side of his head as your wound and his skull was crushed a lot like yours was before the doctors fixed it." Jake hesitated, knowing how weak the connection was, but he certainly wasn't going to tell Ray that he was here because of a dream. "I just thought it was odd that he would be killed that way and then I run into you in the bar that you both frequent."

The Rain Man

Ray seemed nervous. He kept looking around the room and not at Jake. He watched Ray and tried to figure out what he was thinking.

Jake continued. "Since I was curious, I looked up your record at the station. Besides being surprised that you had a record, it also showed you've had a very interesting trend in your arrests."

Ray tried to act nonchalant. He walked to the window sill and picked up a medicine bottle off the table. He looked at it and shook it. It was empty.

"No medicine left. It helps the pain a little bit. I got them from Dr. Evans. It's all gone now and I've got nothing to help me with the pain," Ray said.

Ray suddenly heaved the glass pill bottle at Jake. It hit Jake in the chest and caught him by surprise. Ray ran for the door. Gasping, Jake rolled off the chair and beat Ray to the door to the hall.

"Stop, Ray. I just wanted to question you, but I think we had better do this downtown," Jake said.

"It wasn't me. It was the Rain Man," Ray said as he backed away.

"The Rain Man or Raymond?" Jake asked, remembering the marked out mistake in the police record.

Ray looked terrified. "No! Not me! Never me! It was always the Rain Man!"

"Then why are you worried?"

Ray looked around like a trapped animal. His eyes darted over the entire room. He didn't know what to do. He suddenly screamed.

Jake prepared for an attack, but instead Ray ran and leapt through the window. The glass shattered and the frame cracked as Ray fell outward.

Jake ran to the window.

Ray landed on the porch roof a floor below and rolled down the incline. As he rolled over the edge, he grabbed onto the gutter and let himself hang until he could drop to the street.

"Ray, stop!" Jake yelled.

This was not what Jake had expected to happen. He had thought Ray would be able to explain everything. Now it looked as if Jake's wild hunch might be right in some regard, or maybe Ray simply thought Jake wanted to roust him because of all the run-ins Ray had had with the police.

And if Raymond wasn't the Rain Man, whom was he talking about?

Jake threw open the remains of the window so that he wouldn't slice himself open on a stray piece of glass in the frame. He wasn't desperate enough to jump two stories. He turned and ran out of the room. He couldn't let Ray get away, not after having gotten so close to getting some answers.

Jake ran down the stairs, past the surprised clerk and out the front door. He ran onto the street and looked north and south, hoping that Ray hadn't gotten too far away. He saw Ray running south on Virginia Avenue.

Ray ran down the sidewalk, dodging between pedestrians who were huddled under umbrellas and store awnings. Some were watching the chase, but most of them just wanted to be out of the rain.

Jake considered shooting Ray, but there were too many people in the way. He was forced to chase after him. Jake expected Ray to dive into an alley, but he kept running down the avenue.

Where was he going?

"Stop, Ray! You're only making things worse," Jake called between gasping breaths.

Ray looked over his shoulder and saw Jake. He increased his speed with a burst of energy and turned into an alleyway. Jake followed just in time to see Ray turn south again at another intersection.

As Jake made the turn, he saw a long train creeping across the other side of the road as it pulled out of the rail yard. He thought that the train would be enough to turn Ray either east or west.

Instead of stopping, Ray ran up alongside a train heading into Cumberland. He grabbed hold of a freight car as the train began to pick up speed. Jake considered jumping on another car, but by the time he reached the train, it was moving faster and he was too tired to keep up with the boxcars.

Jake stopped running and bent over to catch his breath as he watched Ray climb into the open box car. Ray stopped to look back at him. Then he ducked inside the box car.

18

Tuesday, March 17, 1936
2:51 p.m.

Raymond watched Jake Fairgrieve turn away from the railroad and head back up Virginia Avenue at a fast walk. Raymond leaned against the side of the box car and took a deep breath. Then the train started into a curve and he lost sight of the policeman.

He looked around the box car and realized he shared it with three hobos. They were sitting cross-legged at one end of the car playing cards on an old crate. With the train in motion, they were relatively safe from the railroad detective and could relax.

"Get away from the bull, did you?" one of the hobos said. He was a large man who looked as if he hadn't shaved in years. He was also as wide across as the other two hobos put together.

Ray nodded and slid to the wooden floor with his back against the wall. He sat next to the door so that he could move quickly if needed.

"Don't let Grady worry you," a second hobo said, nodding toward the larger hobo. The second hobo was a black man. It couldn't be easy being a black hobo since a lot of a hobo's work involved begging and a black man wasn't likely to get much sympathy from white folks. "He's big, but he's got a soft heart. He's not mean like some of the railroad bulls are."

Raymond realized that the three hobos thought he was another hobo who had escaped the railroad detective. They might even have seen him running from Jake.

"Where's this train going?" Raymond asked as he wiped some of the rain from his face and hair.

"Does it matter?" Grady asked.

Did it matter? Raymond couldn't go back to his room. Jake would certainly return there and look around for evidence that Raymond had committed murder.

He would find it, too.

Raymond's life in Cumberland was over. The best that he could hope for was to get to another city and start over.

Inside his head, the Rain Man laughed at Raymond's predicament. *You thought you could talk to her instead of me. I'm with you all the time and she's only with you in your room.*

Raymond rubbed his temples, hoping to ease the pain but knowing it wouldn't. It was the rain. If the rain would stop, so would the pain. He could dull the pain with Dr. Evan's pills and booze, but those were only momentary reprieves. The rain needed to stop, but it just kept falling like it wanted to wash Cumberland and Allegany County off the face of the earth. Maybe he could ride the train to a town that was sunny and warm.

No, the rain is beautiful. It cleanses and washes away sin and memory, the Rain Man said.

"You want to play?" the black hobo said, waving the cards in Raymond's direction.

Raymond shook his head. "No."

The pain in his head was spreading. Running through town hadn't helped any. His blood was pounding through his temples, which only added to the pain.

He tried to concentrate on the vibrations and rolling rhythm of the train. He thought that maybe he could refocus himself so he didn't feel the pain until they reached a place where it wasn't raining. If he could just hold out for a little while longer until the train could take him beyond the rain.

Not likely. The pain is caused by your weakness, not rain.

"I am not weak," Raymond said.

"What did you say?" one of the hobos asked.

"Nothing."

See your weakness? You sit here alone and they will wait for you to sleep. Then they will descend on you and rob you. When they are done with you, they will throw you off this train, the Rain Man warned him.

Raymond looked at the trio of men on the other side of the freight car. They seemed to be engrossed in their game of poker and were ignoring him. They laughed and chatted, barely giving him a glance. But what if the Rain Man was right? Were they dangerous?

No "if" about it. They want what is yours and they think they can take it. They think you are alone, but they don't realize I'm with you.

Despite the Rain Man's optimism, Raymond was still one man.

The Rain Man

They were three men. Even if one of them was no larger than a boy, Grady more than made up the difference.

Raymond looked around. He didn't see anything that he could use as a weapon to protect him against these men. Did they have knives or clubs over in their corner?

It doesn't matter. You have me.

Almost as if it was out of his control, Raymond felt himself standing. He thought about warning the hobos that the Rain Man was coming for them, but he would be warning those who meant to hurt him.

He walked toward them slowly. They didn't notice him until they finished their hand. The black hobo smiled broadly as he pulled the pile of matchsticks toward him. Then they looked up at Raymond.

"Did you change your mind?" Grady asked. "We're all broke so we're playing poker for matchsticks. Of course, given this weather even those are no good if you need a light."

Raymond suddenly kicked the man in the side of the head. When Grady fell over, Raymond stomped on the side of his head. The other two hobos jumped up.

"What are you doing, man?" the black hobo asked.

"Did you think I didn't know what you're planning? You can't fool me," Raymond said.

The hobo shook his head. "You're crazy, man. We don't want no trouble."

The third hobo pulled out a knife. Raymond looked at it and smiled.

"See? I knew what you were planning," Raymond said.

The two hobos separated, trying to get on either side of him. Raymond was more worried about the one with the knife than the black man. Raymond felt the Rain Man take control of him because Raymond was too afraid to fight.

He dodged toward the black man. He grabbed him by the shirt and swung him around into the hobo with the knife. The two men fell together in a heap.

Raymond aimed a kick at the hobo with the knife, hoping to connect with the side of his head. The man rolled to the side and Raymond only managed to stomp the floor of the freight car. He landed so hard that it made his leg tingle. The man took a swipe at Raymond's leg, but Raymond jumped back. The knife only caught the fabric in his pants leg.

The hobos stood up and circled around Raymond.

"You made a big mistake, man," the black hobo said. "You could have played cards and everything would have been fine. Now you've gone and made us mad and hurt our friend."

Grady still hadn't moved. Raymond didn't know if he was dead, but at least he was unconscious. The big man couldn't hurt him.

Raymond said nothing. The Rain Man was in control and the Rain Man didn't talk to anyone but Raymond.

The man with the knife took another swipe at him. Raymond jumped back, but the black man caught him from behind and held his arms behind him.

"Now we gonna gut you like a fish," the black man said quietly.

Raymond swung his head backwards, smashing the man's nose. The black man yelled and let go of him. Raymond spun out of the way of the man with the knife. The man with the knife barely missed stabbing his companion.

Despite the Rain Man's help, Raymond wasn't going to be able to stop the man with the knife and the black man. He had stopped them from hurting him anymore than he already hurt, though. That was the important thing. Raymond was alive and had conquered the pain for the time being.

Raymond saw the open box car door and the scenery rolling by. He was not going to accomplish anything more by remaining here. He ran to the open door and jumped off of the train as the Rain Man gave up control.

He smashed against a hillside that ran near the tracks and rolled over and over to the base of the track bed. The slick rocks scraped his skin and tore his clothes. When he opened his eyes, he could see the wheels of the train rolling only inches away from his face.

Startled, Raymond rolled backwards and sat up. He could still hear the hobos screaming at him from the box car. He had showed them. They wouldn't be picking on any innocent person again anytime soon.

He stood up and looked around. At first, he wasn't sure where he was, but then he recognized the Narrows. The water in Wills Creek had breached its banks and was a raging river filling the Narrows.

Raymond hadn't even gotten out of Cumberland!

19

Tuesday, March 17, 1936
3:12 p.m.

Jake stopped on the porch of the YMCA. He tried to shake the rain from him and made a large puddle at his feet.

A crowd of men waited for him when he walked into the lobby. Eight men of various ages were gathered around the desk clerk, peppering him with questions. When the desk clerk saw Jake, he pointed to him. The men turned to face Jake.

"What's going on?" the dark-haired desk clerk asked.

"That's what I'm trying to find out," Jake replied.

The clerk's eyes narrowed to slits as he stared at Jake. "One of the windows in Raymond's room is busted out, and there's a boy here saying that he saw Raymond fall past his window. Did you throw Raymond out the window?"

"No."

"He wouldn't just jump. There's no way he'd survive."

"Well, he did survive, didn't he? So I guess that means he could jump, too," Jake snapped.

Jake pushed his way through the crowd. He went behind the counter and picked up the phone.

"Hey, that's not for public use!" the clerk said.

"This is not public use. It's official police business," Jake told him.

He picked up the handset and called the station. Bud Seeler answered the phone.

"I hope this is not going to take long, Jake. The flooding has started. Last check, the Potomac was up over 640 feet." It was usually about 630 feet above sea level or lower. "We could use you here as soon as possible," Bud told him.

"Bud, I've got a situation at the B&O YMCA. I think Ray Twigg is involved in the Mark Connelly murder last night. Ray bolted when I tried to talk to him and jumped on a train heading through town about ten minutes ago. I need you to call the railroad and find out where that train is going. Then get the police at the next stop to check out the train and find Ray."

"I'll work on it. I don't think it will take too long. I'm half tempted to ride out of town with him just to get away from all this rain."

"Thanks, Bud. I'm going to search Ray's room now."

"Don't be too long. If it gets any worse, we're going to need you here to help evacuate people and keep the rest from looting."

"I'll try not to be too long."

Jake hung up the phone. He headed for the stairs to take a look at Ray's room. He wanted to see if there was anything incriminating other than Ray's actions.

"Where are you going?" the clerk asked.

"Back up to Raymond's room," Jake said.

"Who's going to pay for the damages to his room?"

Jake shrugged and walked away.

The door to Ray's room was unlocked and Jake stepped inside. Rain blew into the room through the broken window. Jake drew the heavy curtains closed over the window to keep out the rain somewhat. Then he turned on the lamp.

What was he hoping to find? It wasn't as if Jake would find a knife or gun with Ray's fingerprints on them. There hadn't been a murder weapon used against Connelly.

Nothing jumped out at him as being particularly incriminating. He was struck by the fact of how little Ray had. Jake was a bachelor, too, and he had more bowls, pots and pans than Ray.

He saw the arm of a white shirt poking up between the bed and the wall. Jake pulled the bed away and saw a blood-stained shirt jammed down behind the bed. Jake squatted down next to the bed and stared at the shirt. He didn't touch it because he wasn't sure if he would disturb the evidence. He wanted to make sure he had pictures of the scene first. Still, there were some assumptions he could make for the time being.

He was staring at blood and lots of it on the clothes. There were no marks on the wall or bed sheets to indicate that the shirt had been wet with blood when it had been shoved behind the bed. Then Jake recalled how Ray had dried his clothes on the radiator. He could have dried the shirt before he hid it, but why hadn't he washed it free of blood first?

Ray worked for a funeral home. He might have gotten the blood on him from a body there, but that would be easy enough to check out after Jake left here.

He opened the closet door. There were some papers on a top shelf he would read through later to see if he could figure out what was happening with Ray. At the bottom of the closet, a green army blanket had been spread out. Jake moved it aside and staggered backward nearly tripping on the bed.

At the bottom of the closet, curled into a ball, was the body of a woman. She was clothed in a dress with her knees drawn up to her chest. She was middle-aged or so Jake guessed by the clothing. Her face was waxen and wrinkled. From the way she lay on the floor, Jake could also see that her head was oddly dented on the left side.

Why was she here in Ray's closet?

Jake left the room, closing the door behind him. Then he hurried back down to the lobby and called the station again. This time, the desk sergeant didn't even argue with him.

"Bud, things just got a little more complicated here," Jake said.

"I don't need to hear that." Jake lowered his voice so the desk clerk wouldn't hear him. "There's a body here, stuffed into the bottom of his closet. I'm not sure how fresh it is, but it looks like it's in good enough condition to make an identification. I'll take photos, but I need you to call Dr. Rutherford and have him get out here."

"You do know how to spoil a perfectly rotten day," Bud told him.

"Don't I know it."

Jake jogged out to his car to get the camera from his trunk and went back upstairs to Ray's room. He glanced at the clothes and then began to search again. He saw the empty pill bottle on the floor and noted that Chris had prescribed the medicine. Ray had taken Jake's advice and gone to see her.

His eyes were drawn back to the shirt behind the bed. There were three shirt sleeves that he could see.

Three?

That meant that there were at least two shirts back there. Two? Two outfits? Assuming Ray had tossed the clothes he had been wearing when he killed Connelly behind the bed, what did that say about the second damp set of clothes?

Had Raymond killed again last night during the rain?

Jake looked back at the body? Had she been the victim?

Jake wasn't sure why, but he felt that she had been dead longer than a day. She just didn't look like she had been alive recently; something in her complexion made him feel that way. It didn't appear natural.

Did that mean there was still an undiscovered body around someplace?

A chill ran up Jake's spine. He didn't want to be right about that. No one had reported finding a body yet, so maybe Ray hadn't killed someone else.

Or maybe the body just hadn't been found yet.

He looked at the glass pill bottle again. He picked it up. It was empty, but it had only been filled last night. Maybe the medicine also had an effect on Ray's behavior like the liquor he drank. He'd find Chris and ask her about side effects from the medicine.

He took pictures of the body close up and far enough away to show its position in the closet. He also took shots of the rest of the room for a frame of reference.

Daniel Wolford showed up in the room just about the time Jake finished taking his photos. He looked nervous as he came into the room. Wolford shook Jake's hand.

"I expected Dr. Rutherford," Jake said.

"Apparently, he was unreachable so I was called instead since I have some experience with this sort of thing."

"I'm Jake Fairgrieve, Mr. Wolford. I found the body in the closet. I was hoping you might be able to tell me how long she's been dead and how she died."

Wolford walked over to the body and squatted down next to her. He stared at her for a few moments, his brow furrowed in thought. He touched the skin on her hand. At first, Jake thought he was taking her pulse, but Wolford only pressed his fingers into her skin.

"Why doesn't she stink, Mr. Wolford?" McPherson said.

Wolford looked over his shoulder. "She's been embalmed."

"Embalmed?" Jake said. "You mean she was ready to be buried?"

"Perhaps, but I think you won't find any record of her being taken care of at any of the funeral homes in the area," Wolford suggested.

"Do you know who she is?"

Wolford nodded. "I'm surprised you didn't recognize her. There's been some decay, but she's still recognizable. You've probably seen her from time to time. This is Hannah Alt. She was a psychologist at Memorial. I think she had her office not too far from here."

The Rain Man

Jake recognized the name. "But she disappeared two years ago. We had a search out for her for months and never did turn up a hint of where she went."

"Where she went appears to be here," Wolford said.

Hannah Alt had left her office one day in July two years ago and never returned home. Her husband had reported her missing the next morning. No trace of her had been found until today.

"But why?"

Wolford shrugged. "That is your department. I can tell you that she was killed by a blow to the head." He touched the left side of her skull and it bent gently under the pressure of his fingers. "I'll have to look closer to try and tell you what kind of blow she received, but her skull has been reconstructed somewhat here. Not bad work, either."

"Like a funeral director would do," Jake suggested.

"Yes, but as you pointed out Dr. Alt has been missing for two years. No funeral director prepared her for burial or you would have known. We would have had a death certificate, which means that you would have had the body."

"What about Ray Twigg? Could he have done this?"

Wolford stood up quickly. "Raymond lives here?" Jake nodded. "He worked for me for six years until he ran out without a word of explanation earlier today. Yes, he would have the skill to do this job, but why would he embalm a woman and keep her in his room?"

Jake put a hand on Wolford's shoulder and said, "As you said, that's my department and I intend to find out."

20

Tuesday, March 17, 1936
4:05 p.m.

Raymond stood on the porch of a home on Columbia Street and watched the rain fall. He thought about wringing the water from his clothes, but he would just have to go out into the rain again soon. He closed his eyes and rubbed his temples. He couldn't rid himself of the pain as long as the rain continued to fall.

I can show you how to be rid of the pain.

Raymond wasn't sure what frightened him more: The image of what the Rain Man would show him or the fact that he considered giving himself over to the voice again. Whenever he gave into the voice, someone died; the soldier in the army hospital, Dr. Alt, the man in the alley, Dr. Rutherford.

Was it worth ridding himself of the pain?

Why couldn't the rain stop for even a few minutes?

Raymond stepped off the porch and into the rain. It beat at his head like tiny hammers. He headed into downtown Cumberland. He wasn't sure why. He knew he couldn't return to his room at the YMCA. Jake would be watching and waiting for him to return. He was hunting the Rain Man, but he would find Raymond.

It could be Jake. Jake could be the way to relieve your pain and then you wouldn't have to worry about him arresting you, the Rain Man said.

Raymond shook his head. He ran down Columbia Street to Pear Street. Then he turned south on North Centre Street and ran toward town. His running didn't last long. Water swirled around his calves, slowing him down. Not only did he quickly lose his wind, but his head pounded all the more from his exertions.

He needed to find relief without giving into the Rain Man.

He needed his pills. The pills that Dr. Evans had given him were the only things that had brought him some relief. He could get more pills from her and a bottle of whiskey from a bar. Then he could find himself a place in someone's dry basement and wash the pills down with the whiskey. They would bring him some blessed peace. Maybe when he finally woke up from using them, the rain would have stopped and he would be able to think clearly again.

Raymond walked two miles to Dr. Evans office in South Cumberland. She had mentioned to him that she kept afternoon office hours. Hopefully, she would give him more pills. She had to.

Raymond walked inside the office and the nurse receptionist gasped.

"What happened to you?" the woman asked. She was a tall brunette woman who wore a lot of make-up on her average features.

"It's raining."

"Most people would use an umbrella or a rain slicker."

She had a nice smile behind all of her make-up. Raymond would have liked to talk to her if his head hadn't been hurting.

"I can't afford one." He paused. "I need to see Dr. Evans."

"I'll get her. You're in luck. She's had a lot of cancellations this afternoon because of the rain and flooding."

Raymond almost laughed. He could certainly tell the nurse stories of the type of luck that the rain brought him. Absolutely none!

Dr. Evans walked out of her office and stared for a few moments at Raymond. Her red hair was somewhat disheveled and she held a clipboard in one hand.

"Raymond, I'm surprised to see you out in this weather. I thought that you didn't like the rain," she said.

"I don't, but I needed a prescription for the medicine you gave me last night," he said, trying to keep the panic out of his voice.

Her eyebrows arched. "Already? The prescription I gave you should have been good for a couple days at least. What happened to them?"

"The pills helped, but they didn't last that long," Raymond told her.

Dr. Evans held out a hand to him. "I'd better take a look at your head again, Raymond. There may be something I missed earlier, especially if the painkillers I gave you aren't working that well. If we need to, we can go into the hospital for those x-rays I talked about last night."

She led him into her examining room and he sat on the cushioned table. He wasn't surprised that the first place she examined was his head wound. He flinched at her touch. His wounds were very tender right now. He felt as if that side of his head was being pinched and squeezed.

"How have you been, doctor?" Raymond asked.

Dr. Evans smiled at him. "Fine, Raymond. You're the one who's in pain."

"I mean…I was wondering if that man was bothering you anymore."

Dr. Evans stepped back and looked at him. "No, Raymond. I didn't even see Dr. Rutherford when I was at the hospital this morning. I certainly hope you scared him away."

Raymond tried to keep from smiling. "I don't think he'll bother you anymore."

Dr. Evans sighed. "I certainly hope not, but you can never be sure."

"I can."

"I wanted to thank you again for helping me like you did," she said awkwardly.

"You're welcome." Now he did smile. The Rain Man knew how to pay his debts.

Dr. Evans went back to examining him. "You said you received this wound during the war." Raymond nodded. "Have you been seeing a doctor since then?"

Raymond stiffened and wondered if he should tell her about the doctors he had seen and what they had said about him. No. He didn't want her to think less of him.

The phone rang. The nurse answered it and spoke to the caller. A few moments later she stepped into the examining room.

"The call's for you, Dr. Evans. He said it was important." The nurse glanced nervously at Raymond.

"Aren't they always? I'll take it in here, Veronica."

Dr. Evans picked up the phone. "Hello, this is Dr. Evans. Oh, hello. Can I call you back? I'm with a patient right now? What?" She glanced at Raymond. "Are you sure? But he seems so nice." She looked at him again and stepped closer to the door. "Can you come over now? I'm with Mr. Twigg right now, but when I'm done I can see you. Yes. Yes. Goodbye."

She knows what you did. It's in her eyes, the Rain Man told him.

But Raymond didn't need telling. He could see it for himself. Dr. Evans was afraid of him. Someone had just told her some lies about him. Always lies. They always blamed him, never the Rain Man. No matter what Raymond told them.

"Raymond..." she started to say.

Raymond jumped off the table and grabbed her hand. He twisted her arm behind her back and stood behind her with his other hand on her throat.

"You know, don't you?" he whispered in her ear.

"Know what?" she said quickly.

"You know about the Rain Man and what he made me do."

"Who is the Rain Man? What did he make you do, Raymond?"

"That's why I need the medicine, don't you see? It's the only way I can make him go away. I need it," Raymond nearly pleaded with her.

"You need help..."

Raymond nodded vigorously. "I do, and you can give it to me. I need the medicine. It's the only way to quiet the Rain Man."

"I don't understand."

Raymond shook her. "You don't have to understand. You just need to get me more of the medicine you gave me earlier."

"I don't keep it here. It's at the hospital or a pharmacy."

Raymond considered what he could do. Either place was dangerous for him. More people were at the hospital. It would be easier to blend in there. He needed those pills.

"We'll go to the hospital." He let go of her. "Get your coat on."

Dr. Evans put her raincoat on as Raymond watched her. He really didn't want to hurt her because he needed her help. She wasn't going to help him on her own, though. Someone had warned her about Raymond. It must have been Jake, which meant he would be on his way here to arrest Raymond.

Once Dr. Evans had her coat on, Raymond said, "We're going to leave now. No one has to get hurt if you cooperate."

Dr. Evans stared at him angrily. It reminded him of the way she had been staring at the doctor at the hospital yesterday. She thought she was mad at him, but she was really mad at the Rain Man. If Raymond could get his medicine, then she would see that she didn't have to worry about him. He would be calmer. He would be in control, not the Rain Man.

She's not going to help you, the Rain Main warned him.

They walked into the waiting room. Dr. Evans hesitated, but Raymond nudged her forward by pushing her shoulder.

"Are you going out, Dr. Evans?" the nurse asked.

"I, uh,…" she glanced nervously at Raymond. "I need to go to the hospital with Mr. Twigg."

The nurse looked back and forth between Raymond and Dr. Evans.

"What about your appointments?" the nurse asked.

"Tell them I'm not sure when I'll be back. Tell Jake that Raymond has me."

The nurse gasped. Raymond swore as Dr. Evans bolted for the door. He reached out to grab her coat as she moved away from him.

The Rain Man screamed with delight in his head.

Raymond swung Dr. Evans around by the tail of her coat. She fell across the desk and rolled over the desk and into the nurse. Both women fell to the floor.

Raymond ran around the desk. The nurse was screaming. Raymond grabbed her head and slammed it against the floor.

He felt Dr. Evans grabbing at his arms, trying to stop him. She wasn't strong enough, though, when the Rain Man was in control. She was yelling something in his ear, but he couldn't hear her over the Rain Man's shouts of joy.

Raymond pounded the nurse's head against the floor again and again. The nurse stopped screaming. Raymond felt the nurse's head cave in and he stopped slamming her head against the floor. Blood was coming out of the nurse's mouth and nose.

"You killed her," Dr. Evans said.

Raymond spun around and grabbed her by the shoulders. "It wasn't me that killed her. It was the Rain Man. Don't you understand? The Rain Man and you. If you hadn't tried to get her to help you, she would have been all right, but you made her dangerous to me and the Rain Man killed her. It wasn't me."

Dr. Evans stared at the nurse and began to cry.

Raymond jerked her to her feet by her arm. "Get up. We've got to go to the hospital."

"But Veronica…"

"She's dead. You killed her. If you don't want the same thing to happen to you, then you've got to get me that medicine," Raymond told her.

Dr. Evans stumbled across the room in front of Raymond. She stumbled out the front door and into the rain.

21

Tuesday, March 17, 1936
5:13 p.m.

Jake let the phone handset drop back into the cradle. His hand felt numb from gripping it so tightly. Ray was with Chris! He hadn't escaped and left town. He must have jumped off the train before it had gotten too far from town.

Jake left the nearly empty police headquarter and ran outside to his car, which he had parked near City Hall. Chris's office was only a short distance away, and he wanted to get there as quickly as possible.

He couldn't let anything happen to her. It would be on his conscience because he was the one who had set Ray into his panic. He was also the one who had told Ray to go see Chris.

Jake sped along Virginia Avenue to Second Street with water spraying out from either side of the car in large waves. Though there was standing water on Virginia Avenue, he doubted that it would flood here because it was higher up than the downtown area. Whether or not it was official yet, the flooding had started downtown. The roads were underwater even if it was only an inch of water. It meant that the sewers were too full to carry all of the water out of town.

How much more could go wrong?

He needed to approach Ray carefully this time. It was no longer a matter of getting Ray to answer a few questions. Ray Twigg, the innocent country boy soldier, was wanted for murder.

If Ray saw Jake coming, he would run like he had at the YMCA. And that would be the least-dangerous thing he could do. All Jake had to do was remember Connelly's body in the alley or Hannah Alt's body in Ray's closet to know there were worse things Ray could do if he felt threatened. If Chris was close to Ray when Jake arrived, she would be in danger.

Jake parked around the corner from Chris's office and ran through the rain to get to the small building. He didn't see her car parked out front of the brick building. She wouldn't have left when she knew Jake was on the way, and she wouldn't have walked to work in the rain. So had Ray stolen it?

Jake stepped up onto the porch and drew his service revolver. He turned the knob on the door and stepped into the waiting room as quietly as possible. He dropped into a crouch and listened and watched. He heard nothing, but he saw a pair of white-stockinged legs sticking out from behind the desk.

His breath caught because he recognized the legs as female. He ran around the desk and recognized Veronica, Chris's nurse receptionist. The side of her skull had been caved in. Jake didn't have to think long to know who had killed her. Ray had been here.

The first thought that went through his mind was, "At least it's not Chris." Then just as quickly he felt guilty for thinking that. Veronica had been a kind woman who deserved to be mourned.

Why did Ray always kill by trying to crush a person's skull? It certainly wasn't an easy way to kill someone.

Jake rushed into the examining room. It was empty, as he had hoped. At least he hadn't found Chris lying in here with a crushed skull like Veronica.

So where was she?

Her car! If she had gotten away, she would have waited for him. She was the one who had told him to come. Ray must have taken Chris with him for some reason.

Jake grabbed Chris's office telephone and called downtown.

"Bud, you're not going to like this," he said to the desk sergeant.

"What?" He was beginning to sound cranky.

"I've got a dead body at Dr. Chris Evans's office on Second Street."

"Her?"

"No. It's her nurse. Chris's car is missing. My guess is that she's with Ray Twigg in her car. Have everyone keep an eye out for her car. It's a new brown Buick coupe with a hard top."

"What should we do if we find her car?" Bud asked.

"Be careful. Ray Twigg is a murderer. He won't have a gun, but he doesn't need one to kill. We don't want Chris to be his next victim."

"Are you going to wait there for the coroner?"

"No, I'm going to find Ray Twigg. Whatever is driving him to do this is getting worse."

22

Tuesday, March 17, 1936
5:32 p.m.

C hris parked her car in front of Memorial Hospital and turned off the engine. Raymond looked at the brick building and then at her.

"Let's make this quick. We'll just go in, get what you need to stop my pain and then we'll be gone," Raymond told her.

"Where will we go?"

Raymond closed his eyes and rubbed his temples. "I don't know."

"Why don't you let the surgeons decide whether they can help you?" Chris suggested.

Raymond shook his head. "No, it's too late for that now. You doctors just don't learn. At least the Rain Man gives me some relief."

"What do you mean?"

He turned to face her. His voice had an angry tone, but his eyes showed pain and hurt. "You poke. You prod. The Rain Man knows what you're doing. Do you think that he'll let you push him out? No! He'll defend himself. He has before, and because you drive him to kill, you want to punish me!"

Raymond was admitting to killing in a roundabout way. Could he release her now that she had seen him kill Veronica and admitted to it? Or was it more likely Chris would wind up like Veronica? Would he crush her head and leave her corpse lying somewhere it wouldn't be found until it began to stink and decay?

Chris shuddered and then forced her imagination under control. She had to think of what she could do now to save herself.

"There are doctors here who can help you, Raymond. If not a surgeon, there are psychologists," Chris suggested.

Raymond laughed. It was a cold sound without joy. "You're just like the others. I thought you were different. I thought that you could help me."

"I can help you if you let me."

"Then get me my medicine!" Raymond suddenly shouted. The voice was too loud in the car and even more frightening because of the anger it showed.

Chris leaned back against the door, tempted to run. She wondered if she could make it up the stairs before Raymond caught her.

"I won't let the Rain Man win! I've got to stop the pain," Raymond told her.

"Who is the Rain Man?" Chris asked.

"He's the one who's killed all those people. They think I did, but it wasn't me. It was the Rain Man," Raymond nearly whispered.

All those people? How many people had Raymond killed?

"But I saw you kill Veronica." She certainly wished that she hadn't.

Raymond's head whipped around. "You're just like the rest of them. It wasn't me. It was the Rain Man." He leaned closer and tapped the side of his head. "You felt it. That's where he's at."

Chris thought that he might be schizophrenic, but his war wound may have been the cause for his problem. He needed to see a psychiatrist or a surgeon. Maybe both.

"Raymond…" she started to say.

He laid a gentle hand on her arm.

"Don't say anything. I'm in control now, but I don't know how long it will last. Not with this damn rain falling." His grip tightened, then relaxed. "If you're worried about that doctor who bothered you, don't be. The Rain Man took care of him last night."

Took care of. She didn't have to ask for an explanation. She had seen how the Rain Man took care of people. She had seen Veronica.

Did that mean that Vincent Rutherford was dead?

Chris should have been upset at the thought, but she wasn't. She couldn't even muster the least bit of concern that Rutherford had probably been killed as violently as Veronica. That scared her. Did it mean that she had it within her to appreciate what Raymond had done?

She took a deep breath and said, "Okay, let's go to the pharmacy."

She ran up the stairs to avoid being in the rain too long, not to escape Raymond. She didn't want to anger him until she was sure she would be safe and no one else would be hurt.

Surprisingly, Raymond ran past her in an effort to get out of the rain. He waited for her in the doorway to Memorial Hospital.

Poor Veronica! She was dead because Chris had asked her to do a simple task. What kind of man was Chris dealing with? She wanted to cry, but the tears just wouldn't come.

Chris and Ray walked into the hospital and shook the water from themselves. The quiet made her feel even more isolated.

"The pharmacy is this way, but I'll need to write a prescription first," Chris said.

"Let's hurry."

She walked to a nurse's station and picked up a pad from the desk. The nurse on duty watched them, but she didn't say anything. Raymond stood at the door and watched the hallway. Chris wrote out the prescription, but then discreetly lifted the sheet of paper and scribbled another note for help. She couldn't say where she was going from here, but she could say who she was with and that Raymond was dangerous. Hopefully, the nurse could get the police here quickly.

Chris hesitated to hand the pad back to the nurse. She wondered if she was sentencing this woman to a death like Veronica. The nurse took the pad and glanced at the message. Then she looked up at Raymond.

Don't say the wrong thing, Chris pleaded silently.

"I'll call down to the pharmacy and tell them you're on your way," the nurse said.

Chris let out her breath, not realizing she had been holding it. "Thank you."

"Are you done yet?" Raymond asked. He took the prescription and read it. "It's the same thing."

"Of course it is. Do you think I would poison you?"

"I thought you might."

Chris almost wished she had thought to do that, but then Raymond would have caught her. He still hadn't realized she had written an additional note.

"But you said you're not the one I have to worry about. It's the Rain Man," Chris said.

"Yes."

"And the right medicine will help you control the Rain Man."

Raymond nodded. "Yes."

"Then that's what I want to do. I want to help you control the Rain Man."

Raymond smiled.

They walked back down the hallway. Chris tried to smile at the nurses and patients she saw, but she didn't feel that confident. They stopped in front of the pharmacy and Chris passed the prescription to the pharmacist.

"Is this for you?" the pharmacist asked.

Chris shook her head. "This is Mr. Twigg. It's for him. I want to make sure that there's no problem with filling it."

The pharmacist took out a bottle and set it on the counter. Then he typed up the label in a typewriter and pasted it to the bottle. He went back into a locked room and came back out with a large bottle of pills. He carefully counted them out on a board that had a piece of paper laid on it. When he was finished, he rolled up the piece of paper and dumped the pills into the bottle.

The prescription should have been enough to last most people a month, but as quickly as Raymond had used the pills she had given him yesterday, Chris wondered if this would last Raymond a week.

She took the bottle from the pharmacist and passed it to Raymond. He quickly opened it and shook out two pills and popped them into his mouth.

"Raymond, you need to take them with water," Chris said, surprised.

"They seem to work faster this way." He nodded down the hallway. "Let's go."

"Where are we going?" Chris asked nervously.

He didn't answer her as he walked down the hall. Chris reluctantly followed, surprised at her own compliance.

23

Tuesday, March 17, 1936
5:54 p.m.

Jake neared Memorial Hospital in his squad car searching for Chris's car. Just as he had been leaving Chris's office, the phone had rung. He had picked it up, thinking it might be Bud calling him. Instead, it had been a nurse at Memorial Hospital. She had told him about Chris's message and that it had told the nurse to call Chris's office until Jake answered. Then the nurse told him that Chris was with Raymond and that Jake should come to Memorial as quickly as he could.

The roads were shallow rivers as he drove against the current and uphill toward the hospital. The car slid about as if it was on ice rather than in water. Traffic jammed up as cars slowed to get through the flooding streets. Other cars searched for a different way around downtown.

Jake was turning onto Williams Street when he saw Chris's car pass him heading down Williams Street into town. Chris was driving and Raymond sat next to her in the passenger seat.

Jake was tempted to beep his horn, but he realized that might endanger Chris. Instead, he turned left and followed her car down the road. They turned onto Park Street. Jake thought Ray might be heading for Queen City Station to catch a train out of town, but Chris passed the station. She turned left onto Baltimore Street and headed into town.

They were driving into flood waters!

Many of the stores were closed up for the day if not because of the flood then because of the late hour. Doors and windows had been sandbagged to keep the water out. The water surged quickly down Centre, Mechanic and Liberty Streets and spread out into the side streets.

Chris's car suddenly stopped in the middle of the road. The passenger door opened and Ray jumped out of the car. He ran around the car and jerked open the driver's side door. He pulled Chris out.

"Jake!" she yelled.

He'd been seen. Jake stopped his car and jumped out. He was knocked off balance by the swirling water and was swept a few feet down the street before he could get his feet under him again.

He stood up shaking. He wanted nothing more than to get in his car and drive away, but he couldn't leave Chris with Ray.

Jake chased the two of them down Baltimore Street. The going was slow because the water kept getting deeper the closer they moved towards Wills Creek. It was cold water, too. Jake felt his legs beginning to go numb. If he lost his footing now, he would be swept away.

Jake could see Ray running ahead of him. He and Chris weren't that far away, but the water kept Jake from gaining any ground on the two of them.

They turned south on Centre Street, where the current was even faster as the water swept through the city from the north. Jake chased them amid the swirling water.

Ray dodged down an alley, pulling Chris with him. Jake followed. The current let up, but it was still hard to move through the deep water.

Ray crossed Liberty Street and climbed a wall of sandbags and fell into the entryway out of the rain. They entered the six-story Liberty Trust Bank building at the side entrance and disappeared inside.

Jake cursed. Now that he had lost sight of them, they could hide anywhere or they could simply go out another door. He hurried as fast as he could across the deserted street and climbed over the sandbags that were piled seven feet high.

He opened the door and slid through the narrow opening between the door and sandbag wall. Inside, he was surprised to find people in the building since it was after banking hours. It would be harder for Ray to hide if people could see him.

"A man just ran in here with a woman. Where did they go?" Jake asked frantically.

The man pointed to the stairway. Jake bounded up the stairs two at a time, leaving water puddles behind him to mark his path.

On the second floor landing, he stopped and listened. He didn't see anyone in the hallway. He couldn't hear anything other than the falling rain striking the windows.

"Chris!" he yelled, hoping she would answer him.

"Jake, I'm up…"

The Rain Man

Her reply was cut off, but Jake had heard enough. He ran up the stairs. Judging by the sound of her voice, she was nearing the top of the building.

Would Ray try to hide on the roof? There would be nowhere to escape from there. Not even the fire escapes reached that high. Of course, he could drop down to the sixth floor fire escape landing and descend the metal stairs from there.

Although he was sure they were higher, Jake still quickly scanned each floor to make sure he didn't miss Ray or Chris. He didn't want to misjudge and get ahead of them.

On the fourth floor, Jake saw a woman standing in the hallway.

"Did a man and a..." Jake started to ask.

The woman nodded and pointed up. Jake turned and ran. He passed the fifth floor and continued to the sixth. He was about to ask questions of the people on the floor until he noticed the water on the stairs. He looked up and saw the door to the roof was closed, but it must have been opened recently to get the stairs as wet as they were.

Jake ran up the stairs and onto the roof. The rain beat down on his face and he splashed through the puddles on the roof.

"Chris!" he called.

"Jake!"

Jake turned and saw Ray pulling Chris toward the edge of the building. He had to be looking for the fire escape. Jake drew his pistol.

"Stop, Ray!"

Ray looked up. He said nothing, but he pulled Chris in front of him as a shield.

"You can't get off this roof, Ray. You came too high up. There's no fire escape up here," Jake said.

"I don't need a fire escape. I wanted to feel the rain," Ray said.

Feel the rain? Hadn't he had enough of that outside earlier?

Jake said, "Let her go, Ray. It's over."

Ray looked over at him and smiled. "You are no match for me. Even Raymond is no match for me and he lives with me all the time."

Jake didn't like how this was going. He was afraid that Ray might hurt Chris just to spite Jake. She didn't look like she had been hurt so far, but Ray had killed at least three people. He had nothing to lose at this point.

Jake had to separate the two of them, but Ray had a tight grip around Chris's neck.

"Raymond, it's over now. Let me help you get better. I can make sure you are taken to a good hospital. I'll help you," Chris said.

Raymond shook her. Chris winced in pain.

"I don't need a hospital!" he yelled. "I need the rain and the freedom it gives me. I won't let him confine me. Raymond is weak, but the Rain Man is strong."

"But you two are the same."

"We are not!"

Jake shifted his position. He had to stay between Ray and the stairwell, but he also didn't want Ray to get too close to the edge of the building. It was a long way down. Ray shifted his position to keep Chris as his shield.

"Let her go, Ray. You aren't getting off this roof," Jake warned him.

"You've lost and you don't even know it. This is my domain. With the rain, I have power. I won't be stopped. I can't be stopped," Ray said.

"Don't be so sure of that."

Jake shot at the low parapet behind Ray. The bullet hit the brick and sprayed shards against Ray's legs. Ray jumped and glanced at his legs. He was so startled that he loosened his grip on Chris.

"Chris, drop!" Jake ordered.

For once, she did what he asked without arguing. Ray looked up to see that he no longer had a shield and without hesitation, flung himself backwards off the roof before Jake could shoot.

Ray fell over the edge without screaming.

Jake ran to the parapet. By the time he looked over the edge, all he could see was the foam and ripples from where Ray had fallen into the water. He waited to see if Ray surfaced. A minute passed. The foam dissolved and the ripples merged with the current.

Even if Ray had somehow managed to survive his impact with the water, the shock of the cold water would have killed him.

Still, Jake waited with his pistol pointed at the water.

"Is he gone?" Chris asked.

She was standing beside him and slightly back from the edge.

"I think so. It's hard to know. The current will probably wash his body into the river. We may never find him," Jake told her.

"I wonder if a psychiatrist could have helped him."

Jake thought about Hannah Alt, the dead psychiatrist. "I think one may have tried."

"It didn't help," Chris noted.

"No, it didn't," Jake agreed.

Jake slid his arm around Chris and pulled her close to him. She was shivering.

"Let's go get you dried off," he said.

They walked back to the stairwell.

24

Tuesday, March 17, 1936
6:49 p.m.

Chris shivered so hard that her teeth chattered. Jake hugged her and rubbed her arms and back. She needed to be warm and dry. Of course, blankets were hard to come by in a bank.

Jake looked out the window at the sandbag wall. He stepped outside the door and looked over the wall. The water had to be at least six feet deep now and it was still raining. Would the flood waters breach the sandbag wall?

Everyone stranded in the bank had begun moving from the ground floor up to the second-floor offices in case the sandbags gave way. Jake and Chris joined them.

"I've got to get you back to your house so you can get into some dry clothes," Jake said.

Chris shook her head. "No, not my house. My father...he won't be able to help."

Jake thought for a moment and said, "Don't worry about help. I know someone who can help if I can get you to her house."

Outside, someone in a rowboat paddled by, fighting the current. The boat was moving against the current at the pace of a slow walk. The boater helped two people from a second-floor window across the street into the boat and then floated away with the current.

Jake saw another boat moving down the flooded street. He opened the window and leaned out, waving his badge at the man. The boater maneuvered his rowboat over to the bank building. He grabbed hold of the sill to steady the boat.

"I've got a woman in here I've got to get out," Jake said.

"We're taking people to the armory where the Red Cross can look after them. They've got cots, blankets and food there," the boater said.

"How's Columbia Street?"

"Fine, as far as I know. It sits kind of high so it won't flood probably unless things get really bad. West Side's cut off unless you want to chance crossing the creek on the railroad viaduct."

That meant Jake wouldn't be going home for awhile. It also meant that even if Chris had wanted to go home, she was also stranded on this side of Wills Creek until the flood waters receded.

"How close can you get us to Columbia?" Jake asked.

"Not too close. I'm out here because you guys called for help to rescue anyone stranded, which isn't too easy with such a strong current. I can get you up to George Street. That's where the water gets too shallow for the boat. You'll have to make your way from there," the boater explained.

Depending on where on George Street the man dropped them off, it probably meant they would have a half-mile or so walk to his sister's house on Columbia Street. Still, Jake wasn't going to get a better offer. Maybe he could flag down a car on Henderson if cars were still getting through on the road.

He helped Chris into the boat and then climbed in.

"Where are we going?" Chris asked.

"My sister's," Jake said.

"Why can't we go back to the cars?"

"They're probably stuck in water by now. The water's higher now than when we went into the bank," Jake explained.

Jake picked up a paddle and helped the man turn the boat around. The current wasn't as fast on Baltimore Street because it ran east to west while the water came from the north. They were working against the current and it would take some time to reach Henderson.

Jake's shoulders ached from paddling the rowboat, but he knew that if he let up, the current would ram the boat against the buildings on Baltimore Street. They passed their stranded cars. Water splashed across the hood on the cars. Even as Jake watched, the water pushed Chris's car sideways and up against the old Citizen's Bank building. As they neared George Street, the land sloped upwards and the water shallowed out. The current lightened.

Jake jumped into the water. It came up to his knees. He grabbed hold of the boat to pull it onto the ground.

"I can get you in a little closer," the boater said.

"No. You've got work to do. We can manage from here," Jake said.

He lifted Chris out of the boat. She was still shivering. The rain certainly wasn't helping any.

The boat backed away from them as the current took hold of it. Chris waved to the boater.

"Thank you," Chris said.

"My pleasure, ma'am. You take care of yourself," he replied.

Jake carried Chris across the railroad tracks, but he set her down on Henderson Boulevard because his arms were aching and the water was only ankle deep there. They would be able to move quicker with both of them walking.

"Jake, I need to tell you about Raymond," Chris said.

"I know all I need to know about Ray."

"He murdered Veronica right in front of me," she said hesitantly.

"I know. I saw her when I got to your office. I called the morgue."

"I only asked her to call for help and he killed her," she said more to herself than Jake.

"He also was the one who murdered Mark Connelly."

"He kept talking about the Rain Man as if it was somebody else."

Jake nodded. "Yes, but he is the one who committed the murders."

"Physically, yes, but was it Raymond mentally?"

"What are you talking about?"

Jake noticed a change in her voice. It steadied as she took on her professional tone. "He kept complaining about the pain in his head making him allow the Rain Man to control him. He was afraid of that happening and he was afraid of the rain. What if the rain caused him pain like it does with people with arthritis? This is a bad storm, it would hurt him a lot more than a typical storm."

"Are you saying the rain drove him crazy?"

Chris shook her head. "No, I think he was already crazy. This just brought out the crazy side of his personality. The Rain Man. Raymond. Don't you hear the similarity in the names? They are two sides of the same coin. Raymond and the Rain Man"

Jake thought about Hannah Alt and had to agree. Ray had already been crazy before the storm. Not that it excused him from what he had done. At least three people were dead. Ray needed to be stopped.

"Is he dead?" Chris asked.

"I think so. Six stories is a long way to fall."

"It was only five stories with the flooding."

"That's still a long way." Jake shook his head. "I just don't know for sure, but I have to say, yes, he's dead."

They walked down Henderson Boulevard and then up Bedford

Street for a block until they turned onto Columbia Street near the Columbia Street School. People were in the streets, heading for the flooded areas to try and help. Some were headed to the churches for refuge. Other people were on their porches watching out for their own homes in case the flooding reached this high.

"Tell me where we are going again," Chris asked.

"My sister's house. It should be dry and she can take care of you until everything quiets down," Jake told her.

"I have to get back to my father at some point."

"I'll check in on him as soon as I can and make sure he's all right," Jake promised.

His sister's house was a two-story house with yellow wooden siding and white trim. His sister and her children were sitting on the front porch watching the rain and the flooding as were many other people. Jake's brother-in-law was missing. He would be out working with the fire department to help get people out of the flooded areas.

"Jake, what are you doing here?" Virginia called.

"Chris spent some time in the water. She needs to get into some dry clothes before she catches pneumonia. It wouldn't hurt to warm her up, either," Jake said as he led Chris onto the porch.

"So this is the mysterious Dr. Evans," Virginia said as she looked Chris over. "Well, let's get you in the house next to the fireplace and into some dry clothes. Mine should fit you."

"Why did you call me mysterious?" Chris asked.

"Because I've heard about you from my big brother, but he hasn't bothered to invite me over to meet you. I've even considered getting sick just so I could meet you."

Chris looked over her shoulder at Jake, but he just shrugged as if to say it was out of his control. He knew Virginia would watch over Chris, though, if nothing more than to pry information about their relationship from her.

Jake watched them go inside. He walked back to the edge of the porch and looked out on the street. There was standing water on the street here, but it wasn't too bad. The house was high enough that it probably wouldn't flood. Many others would, though.

"You're all wet, too, Uncle Jake," Jessica said as she came out onto the porch with him.

Jake shook his head. "This is still a work day for me, and as you can see, I'm going to be busy, Squirt."

"Like Daddy?"

Jake nodded. "Yea, I suppose so."

He hoped that his rushing around to try and find a killer was finished. Now he would just have to worry about keeping people from drowning.

25

Tuesday, March 17, 1936
6:50 p.m.

The rainstorm engulfed Raymond. The water swirled around him in his eyes, his mouth, and his ears. And yet in those moments when he expected the pain in his head to be at its worst, it was gone. Raymond almost welcomed the water and its soothing touch.

Its chill numbed him, but the cold also brought him peace, and how he so wanted peace and freedom from pain. Raymond gave himself over to the water and allowed the cold to numb his pain. He allowed the water to fill him.

Then he felt himself being hauled out of the water. His eyes were open and he saw the water recede from him, slaking away like night giving way to morning. He saw air and the evening sky. Again, the rain hit his face, though he could barely feel it because of the numbness throughout his entire body. The water was still protecting him.

"Hold on, buddy!" an unseen person said. "I need blankets! This guy feels like an ice cube."

"Is he alive?" another person asked.

Their words sounded as if they were coming from far away rather than right next to him.

"He seems to be, but we'd better get him to the armory. They've got nurses and doctors there. He needs help now. He can't wait for a full boat," the first man said.

Raymond felt himself lifted out of the water. He was dumped into a boat on his back and had a blanket wrapped around him. He thought that he could actually feel some of the water leaving him as the blanket absorbed it. If he could have formed more tears, he would have cried. He didn't want the water to leave him. It welcomed and protected him.

Raymond saw his two rescuers. One was a red-headed teenager. The second was an older man with a black beard and mustache. The older man began rubbing Raymond's arms.

"Give him a good rubdown, Bobby. We've got to make sure his blood keeps moving. He's beginning to turn blue," the older man said.

Bobby followed the older man's lead and soon Raymond began to feel a slight warmth and tingling in his arms.

"Hang on, buddy," the older man said. "We'll get you to some help."

Raymond thought that he tried to tell them to throw him back into the water and give him the peace that he wanted, but his body didn't respond to his thoughts. His mouth wouldn't move. He was a statue.

"I'm surprised he's alive," Bobby said.

"That may change real soon unless they can get him into a warm bath at the armory."

Yes! A bath had water. That is what Raymond wanted.

"Get us to the armory," the older man said. "I'll keep working on him."

Raymond felt the rain on his face as the teen moved away. If it was still raining, the pain would return. The Rain Man would return.

Raymond cried tearlessly, but no one could tell because of the rain. The Rain Man was attacking him and forcing his compliance.

Then he slipped into the darkness.

He felt warmth spread throughout his body and he opened his eyes. The sun was bright and Raymond squinted to see where he was. He sat cross-legged in the middle of a desert.

The pale sand was hot beneath his hands. He clenched his hands, grabbing at the dry sand. Dry. He let it trickle between his fingers. It looked like rain, but it was dry.

Blessedly dry! Dry rain!

Raymond laughed. His pain was gone. The world was dry and Rain Man was gone. Raymond was free!

He stood up. The sand shifted dangerously beneath his feet, but Raymond kept his balance. He was tempted to brush the sand from his clothes, but then he decided to leave it on him as a reminder that the Rain Man no longer had power over him.

Raymond looked around, wondering where he was. Which way should he go to reach a town? All he could see in any direction was sand and sun.

To the west, the heat bounced off the sand and shimmered in a way that reminded Raymond of a river running. It chilled him to think of water, but he knew that water would not survive long in the desert.

The shimmering heat waves moved closer and Raymond thought he could see a person in them. He squinted to make out who it was. As the person moved closer, the heat waves didn't disappear and Raymond was suddenly scared. He had seen heat waves bounce off the streets in the middle of a hot summer day, and they always vanished when he moved close to them. The man hidden within the waves walked directly toward him and Raymond backed away.

"Worried, Raymond?" the person said.

Raymond recognized the voice. It was the Rain Man.

"No, you're gone. You can't survive here. There's no rain, no water."

"But where is here?" the Rain Man asked.

"It's a desert."

"But where is the desert?"

Raymond didn't know where the desert was. He couldn't remember how he had gotten here, only that he was here and that it was a refuge, or at least he had thought it was a refuge from the Rain Man.

"It doesn't matter where the desert is, only that it is a desert and you have no power over me here," Raymond replied.

The Rain Man laughed. The heat waves still surrounded him and Raymond realized that they weren't heat waves but actually water that clung to the Rain Man.

How could that be? He was tempted to reach out and touch the water that hung suspended in the air.

"I have power here because here is still within your mind," the Rain Man said.

Raymond shook his head furiously. "No."

"You can't escape me, Raymond. You are me and I am you. There is no escaping your fate," the Rain Man told him.

Raymond turned and ran. He tried to run over the sand dune he was standing next to, but he slipped halfway up and fell to his knees.

The Rain Man continued to walk toward him, laughing as he moved.

Raymond tried to stand again, but he couldn't get his balance on the shifting sands. It kept moving out from under his feet.

Why didn't the Rain Man fall?

He just kept walking toward him. He was only a yard behind Raymond. He screamed and began to crawl up the hill.

Then the Rain Man was on top of him, and Raymond felt the rain surrounding the Rain Man beat down on his entire body.

"You are mine," the Rain Man said.

Raymond woke up and felt hands pushing him down. He looked up and saw a black-haired nurse leaning over him, pushing down on his shoulders.

"Calm down, sir. You're all right," the nurse said.

She looked worried. Maybe he wasn't all right. How could he be if the Rain Man had taken him?

The nurse pressed him back against the cot. Raymond relaxed and fell back against the cot. What could he do? He took a deep breath and smelled the dampness in the air. He hadn't escaped the water and flooding.

"Where am I?" Raymond asked.

"The state armory. Some of the rescuers who are out bringing in families who have been flooded out brought you in. You nearly froze and drowned. The Red Cross is helping take care of everyone here."

He was dry now at least. That was something, but Ray had learned that even dryness could shelter the Rain Man.

"Who's here?"

The nurse shrugged. "There are hundreds of people here and more keep coming in all the time. The rescuers, the fire department and the police are bringing people in all the time."

Police! Jake Fairgrieve!

Raymond tried to sit up again, but the nurse pushed him back again.

"You need to rest. You nearly froze to death," the nurse warned him.

"I need to leave."

"You can't. You can't get through downtown. It's a river. The rescuers are having trouble getting around. There's even water around the armory now."

Raymond shook his head. He couldn't stay here. It wasn't safe. Jake would find him. Jake was probably coming here to find him now.

With a surge of panicked strength, Raymond pushed the nurse away and rolled off the cot. The nurse yelled as she fell onto the floor and against another cot. He stood up on shaky legs. They still felt somewhat numb, but at least he could move.

He was barefoot, but someone had dressed him in dry clothes. They weren't what he had been wearing earlier in the day, though. He grabbed his wallet off the bed and staggered forward as another nurse came toward him.

They know. They want to hold you here so Jake can get you, the Rain Man said.

Raymond saw it now. The Rain Man was right. These people didn't want to help him. They wanted to keep him here until Jake came. They had probably already called him to tell him where Raymond was, just like Dr. Evans had done.

Raymond punched the second nurse in the face. She fell to the floor holding a bloody nose and screaming. Someone beside him yelled, but Raymond ignored him.

"No! The Rain Man told me what you're trying to do," Raymond shouted.

He looked around for the nearest door out of the armory. When he saw it, he also saw people starting to move toward him. He ran between the rows of cots. His legs threatened to give out on him, but he knew that he couldn't stop. If he stopped, they would catch him and hold him for Jake.

Inside his head, the Rain Man laughed so loudly that Raymond wanted to cover his ears.

He upended an empty cot and threw it at the group beginning to gain ground on him. The people stumbled over the cot and each other, allowing Raymond to widen the gap between them.

"You won't catch me! The Rain Man will help," Raymond yelled.

A man lying on a cot reached out for him and Raymond kicked him, knocking him out of the cot. The man grunted as he tumbled onto the floor.

Then Raymond ran through the door and into the rain outside.

The Rain Man screamed with joy.

26

Tuesday, March 17, 1936
8:11 p.m.

Jake walked across the railroad tracks at the Knox Street crossing and headed back into town. The rain pelted him, but he was beyond feeling the cold in the rain, only the wetness. He didn't even shiver any longer.

He wanted to get to police headquarters to see where he was needed in helping with damage control from the flooding. He would have to file a report about Ray Twigg, too, but that could wait until the flood waters receded. Right now, the danger was from the flood. It endangered lives, damaged property and hindered the efforts of rescue workers. There would be plenty of work to do until he was able to walk down Baltimore Street again. He had already seen some of the other officers moving about town and trying to help where they could.

As Jake neared City Hall, he noticed the building was dark. He couldn't even see the windows of the police headquarters on the ground floor. It was washed out and completely underwater. He hoped that Bud and the rest of the crew had finished moving the files up to the first floor. Jake shook his head. The police weren't operating out of City Hall. So where were they calling headquarters for the duration of the flood?

City Hall looked like a mountain rising out of the ocean. Jake wondered if he would even be able to wade to it. The water was getting deeper with every step he took.

He remembered wading through flood waters with Melissa and how he had felt so out of control when he had lost his balance and been swept away into the churning river.

He found a nearby call box and used his key to open the protected phone that the police used to communicate with headquarters when they were on the street and needed help. He picked up the receiver and heard nothing. The flood must have taken the phone lines down, leaving the city without an easy way to coordinate its rescue efforts. Jake closed up the call box and looked around.

He could see boats out on the water, moving people from flooded areas to dry ones. It seemed like people were beginning to worry that the second floors of their buildings would flood. This was going to be worse than the 1924 floods.

He watched an armchair and wooden door caught in the current float past him.

How much damage would this flood leave behind? Any amount would be too much for most people. Money wasn't plentiful right now. Certainly not the amount of money it would take to rebuild a house. He had already seen one home on Mechanic knocked off its foundation by the flood waters.

Jake carefully moved deeper into the water and flagged down a boat by waving his arms and yelling. Two men paddled a rowboat over to him.

"Are you in trouble?" one of the men asked.

Jake recognized him. It was Harvey McIntyre.

"Harvey, what are you doing out here?" Jake asked.

"Me and my boy are helping out where we can. We've got our fishing boat, and we're putting it to good use. You should see the big ones we're catching," Harvey joked. It seemed like nothing could take away his sense of humor.

Jake smiled. "That's good because I can use your help."

The two men hauled him into the boat. The other man was Harvey's teenage son, Bennett.

"What are you doing to help?" Jake asked.

"We're just moving back and forth helping out everyone who's stranded on a second floor and getting them to the armory or onto higher ground," Harvey said.

"Where are the police working out of?" Jake asked, nodding toward the building.

"I guess there's a few still in City Hall. Power's been out there about an hour. Most everybody's moved to higher ground and the police and firemen are pretty much doing what you're doing...getting by on their own," Bennett said.

The boat was large enough to hold eight people, which meant they could pick up five more people as they moved through the flooded streets.

"Where are you taking everyone once you pick them up?" Jake asked.

"It depends. If they live in town and don't have a home anymore, we take them to the armory. The Red Cross has set up there and its filling up pretty fast. Otherwise, we take them to the edge of the flooding so they can make their way home on their own."

"Isn't the armory flooded?"

Harvey shook his head. "Not yet. They put a sandbag wall around the outside and the main floor's high enough to be above the water."

Jake was still uncertain. "That's still taking a chance."

"I suppose so, but what's the alternative? The hotels that are dry are full. We were trying to get people to Emmanuel's parish house since it's close and high on the hill, but the bridge is covered and it's not safe to cross." Harvey glanced over his shoulder. The steeple of Emmanuel Episcopal Church could be seen above the nearby buildings.

They paddled down what had been Bedford Street and turned into the current going down Liberty Street. Harvey and his son kept their paddles in the water to slow their progress down the road.

"Keep your eyes on the water, too. There have been a few people we've had to fish out. They're the important ones. If they're in this water too long, they can get hypothermia," Harvey told Jake.

"You don't have to tell me," Jake said. "I've been wading through a lot of this and I know it's cold."

Bennett pointed to a man and woman standing on top of the marquee for the Liberty Theater that announced Ann Harding was starring in "The Lady Consents." They began to move the rowboat to the side to help the couple. The boat slammed up against the marquee, smashing some of the light bulbs. If there had been power to them, it would have electrified the water around the marquee and made it even deadlier.

Jake reached up and held out his hands to help the two people into the boat.

"Thank you," the man said. "We were moving equipment up to the second floor to keep it dry, but then we got caught ourselves."

"We're glad to be of help," Harvey said.

"Where do you live?" Bennett asked.

"We live on Mechanic Street, the 400 block," the woman said.

"Not anymore you don't."

"What's that mean?" the woman asked.

The Rain Man

"Take a look around you, ma'am. Mechanic Street is right next to Wills Creek. It was one of the first streets to flood. All of the homes along it are nearly under water," Bennett said. Jake thought that Bennett could have been more tactful, but the teenager was probably tired if he had been working long in this mess.

The woman registered her shock as what Bennett was saying sunk in. Her mouth parted as if she was going to say something, but she began to sob. The man put his arm around her and hugged her.

"Where are we going to go then?" the man asked.

"We'll drop you off at the armory. The Red Cross will take care of you until things get back to normal," Harvey said.

The man nodded and whispered something to his wife.

"Do you think it will keep raining another day?" Jake asked.

"If it does, I'll start looking for an ark because there won't be anything left of this town," Harvey said without a hint of humor.

27

Tuesday, March 17, 1936
9:21 p.m.

Raymond plunged into the waist-high cold water. He alternated between swimming with the current and wading until he lost his balance tottering on his numb legs. The water spread out more as it moved through town and was losing some of its power and depth.

His head ached constantly. He recognized it now as the Rain Man's presence. Raymond needed to find a way to stop the pain so he could think about what he should do.

I will tell you what to do. Trust me, the Rain Man said.

Raymond either needed more of those pills that Dr. Evans had given him or booze and lots of it. He stood up and felt in his pockets for his pill bottle that he had gotten at Memorial Hospital. Then he remembered that he wasn't wearing his clothes. The people at the armory had changed him into dry clothes after they had hauled him out of the water. He had lost one way to relief.

He would have to find a bar then. Booze took longer to work than the pills, but it worked.

Raymond slogged through the water heading for South Cumberland. He would find a way to tame the Rain Man. Then he would find a way out of Cumberland and Allegany County. Maybe he would cross the Potomac River into West Virginia and head south.

A rush of current swept Raymond off his feet. He fell backwards and under the water. The current pushed him sideways and turned him around. He rolled and spun under the water. Suddenly, he wasn't sure which way was up. He held out his hands, hoping to either feel the flooded street or feel a breeze of air. He couldn't feel anything. How could that be? There had to be a bottom. There had to be a surface.

He moved his arms more frantically, but the water slowed his movements.

The Rain Man

Inside his head, the Rain Man laughed. *So you thought that the water would protect you. It is simply a different master.*

Raymond's hand hit something solid near his right side. It was the brick paving on the street! He was lying on his side!

Raymond righted himself and put his feet on the street. Then he launched into the air. His head broke the surface and Raymond sucked in the night air. For once, he did not mind the rain as long as there was air between the raindrops.

He settled back down and swam with the current until the water became only a few feet deep. He got his feet under him again. The water swirled around his knees. As Raymond walked onto solid ground, he saw a man sitting on the front porch of his house watching him make his way through the water.

"Looks like you fought the flood and the flood won," the man said.

Raymond wiped the water from his eyes and looked over at the man sitting in the shadows. He was an old man with thick glasses that made his eyes appear as large as half dollars.

"I fell in back around Baltimore Street. I've been trying to get out since then," Raymond said.

"What are you doing out in this weather anyway? Were you trying to gawk at all this mess? It serves you right if you fell in," the man asked.

"I was helping with the rescue efforts," Raymond lied. "I was trying to fish someone out of the water and I fell out of the boat and got swept away."

Raymond moved onto the man's small front lawn, though it was more like swampland. Still, there was no chance of the current sweeping him away.

"You wouldn't have a bottle or two around, would you?" Raymond asked. "I could certainly use something to warm me up."

The man shook his head. "Can't help you there. My wife doesn't abide with having liquor in the house. I've got some fresh coffee that's nice and hot. You're welcome to that."

Raymond considered it. The coffee would certainly warm him, but it wouldn't do anything to drive the Rain Man out of his head. Being rid of the Rain Man was more important than being warm.

"Thank you for the offer, but I think I'll make my way home and get some dry clothes on there," Raymond said.

He turned and slogged off up the hill on Oldtown Road toward where Virginia Avenue and Maryland Avenue met. He wasn't planning on heading back to his apartment, but he was sure he could find a bar that was open. South Cumberland wasn't flooded like downtown. The businesses here wouldn't have closed because of the rain.

He swerved into the first place he found, a small dive at the intersection of First Street and Virginia Avenue called Tam's. He opened the door and stepped inside, dripping rain and river water.

"There's another one you'll have to run through the wringer, Tam," someone in the bar said.

"Stand in the tub until you get your coat and shoes off," the bartender said. Raymond assumed the man was Tam.

Raymond obediently stood in the large, wooden tub and let himself drip into the bottom of the tub.

"I don't have a coat," Raymond said.

The bartender leaned over the bar. "You were out in this mess without a coat or umbrella?"

"I didn't have much of a choice. I got caught in the flood and swept through the new Cumberland River," Raymond lied.

"You were caught in all that?" Tam said, pointing out the window.

Raymond nodded.

"Well, I can see how you would need a drink after that."

"I hope you don't mind wet money."

"As long as it's American, I'll take it anyway I can get it."

Raymond walked over to the bar and sat down.

"Then you'd better bring a bottle because there's a lot about today that I want to forget," Raymond said.

The bartender sat a bottle of Kessler's Private Blend Whiskey in front of him. "Amen to that."

28

Tuesday, March 17, 1936
9:47 p.m.

The rowboat grounded near the Maryland National Guard Armory on South Centre Street. Bennett McIntyre jumped out and pulled it further up against the cement stairs so that it wouldn't float away in the fast-moving current. Harvey tied a rope to the metal railing to secure the boat. He didn't leave any slack in the rope because the current immediately tried to pull the boat away from the stairs. Inside the boat, Jake helped the couple from the Liberty Theater onto the stairs.

"Let's get you inside. They'll take care of you until the flood passes," Jake said.

The couple didn't say anything. They nodded numbly. The woman was still sniffling. Neither one had said anything since they had realized that their house might be destroyed or at least badly damaged.

Jake led the couple into the armory. A nurse at the door wrote down their names and showed the man and woman to two available cots. She spoke quietly to them and sounded truly sympathetic.

Jake looked in the arena area. It was now the temporary home to hundreds of people displaced by the flood. Hundreds of cots spread out all over the floor with barely any room between them to walk. People ate warm meals and gathered in small clusters. No one looked like they would be getting any sleep this evening.

"How is it going here?" Jake asked one of the Red Cross volunteers.

"For the most part, good. Most people are cooperative. I think a lot of them are still in shock at losing their homes in the flood."

"Do you need more help?"

He was thinking that Chris and Virginia would probably be willing to volunteer here to help where they could.

The volunteer shook her head. "No, it's already getting pretty crowded in here. We may actually need to find another place to start taking people. The problem is that we can't call around to find out what's available because the phones are out. WTBO is saying that all of the hotels outside the flooded area are full."

"What about using the third floor and up of the Fort Cumberland Hotel?" Jake suggested.

"We may do that, but we'd have to transport these people there against the current. That's hard enough, but some of these people had a hard time before they got here. Some even saw their homes swept away. They'll get hysterical if we try to take them out into the flood again."

"I'm with the police. I might be able to talk to someone so you could use the upper floors of City Hall," Jake offered.

"That's fine, but there's still the problem with getting people there and how they will react. In fact, I wish you had been here earlier. A police officer would have been a big help."

"How so?"

"We had a man in here who went a bit mad with grief. He was hitting people and yelling," the aide explained.

"What happened to him?" Jake asked.

"He ran outside, yelling something about a rain man. If he didn't want to stay, we weren't going to keep him. He was too dangerous and he was upsetting some of the others."

Rain Man. Jake stopped walking. There couldn't be two people who ranted about a Rain Man. He had thought Ray was dead. How could he have survived the fall from the Liberty Trust Building? Five floors! He hadn't surfaced after he had fallen.

"This man who ran out, what did he look like?" Jake asked.

"His most-obvious feature was that his head leaned to one side. He was medium height with brown hair. He was pretty thin. He was a heavy drinker. You could tell by his nose. He was pretty close to drowned when the rescuers brought him inside. We used warm-water bottles to bring his body temperature back up," the volunteer recalled.

"Do you know his name?"

Jake already knew the man's name. He couldn't imagine anyone else in town yelling about the Rain Man, but he wanted to hear the name Ray Twigg just to know he wasn't crazy.

"We didn't have time to ask his name since he was unconscious when he was brought in. If he hadn't regained consciousness, we would have sent him onto the hospital. We have his clothes, though. We gave him back his wallet when we redressed him."

Ray had survived the fall. Five stories down into six feet of water.

If he could survive that fall, what else could he do?

Jake had thought Ray was crazy to jump, but Ray had lived through the fall. Jake still thought Ray was crazy, but he also realized that there was no way he could anticipate what Ray might do.

How could he find him? Who was the Rain Man?

Chris felt that it was the rain driving Ray mad. So as long as it was raining, Ray would be out of control. He would be dangerous to anyone he met.

"Did anyone see where he went?" Jake asked.

"We followed him out these doors. He ran into the water and swam south with the current. We just wanted to make sure that he left us alone, so we didn't follow him."

Jake ran back outside and jumped in the rowboat. Harvey and Bennett were eating sandwiches given to them by the Red Cross staff.

"What's the rush?" Bennett asked.

"I need you to paddle as fast as you can as far down this street as you can," Jake said.

"What's wrong?"

"Police business. I'm after a killer and he's going that way." Jake pointed down the street.

They untied the rowboat. It slipped into the current and they started down the street.

29

Tuesday, March 17, 1936
10:29 p.m.

The rain's stopped."

Jake blinked at the words not fully comprehending them at first. Stopped? It had been raining for more than a day. He had begun to think that it would never stop.

He lifted his chin and stared into the night sky. Nothing on his face. Jake smiled.

"I guess that means the water will be dropping soon," Bennett McIntyre said.

"Then the real work begins. You were just a toddler during the twenty-four floods. You don't remember what kind of mess a flood leaves behind," Harvey told his son.

The rain had stopped. Nature's fury had been vented on the region. That was all Jake cared about now.

Harvey stuck an oar in the water until it struck bottom. It was barely covered with water. He withdrew it and shook his head.

"We're not going any further in this direction," Harvey said to Jake.

Jake stood up in the rowboat and looked around. He could see water and buildings, but he couldn't see Ray. Where had he gotten to? They couldn't be that far behind him.

"You lose something?"

Jake turned and saw the old man sitting in the shadows of his porch. He was sipping a hot cup of something. Jake could see the steam rising from the cup.

"Did you see someone swim by here within the last half an hour or so?" Jake asked the man.

The old man stood up and walked to the railing of his porch. "I've seen a lot of things float by here tonight. Armchair. Piano. Car. And people."

"Was one of those people a man?"

The old man nodded. "He was."

"Did you talk to him?"

"I did indeed. He said he got washed into that river there while trying to help rescue people stranded in town," the old man said.

That didn't sound like Raymond unless the man was lying.

"Was he a thin man with brown hair and a lopsided-looking head?" Jake asked.

"I'm not sure about his hair, being it's the middle of the night and dark out, but he was thin and his head did seem to lean to the right."

"That's him," Jake said. "Can you tell me where he went? I'm trying to find him."

"He asked for a drink and not the type I'm holding, if you get my meaning," the man said as he held his cup out toward Jake. "I offered him coffee, but he turned me down. He walked away."

"Did you see where he went?"

"The last I saw he was heading up Oldtown Road. I guess it would be pretty easy for him to find a drink there."

Jake turned to Harvey. "I'm going to leave you here. I've got to go after Ray."

"Do you want some help? I'm still good in a fight," Harvey offered.

Jake shook his head. He wasn't too sure he wasn't making a mistake. Who knew what a man with the stamina to survive a five-story fall and driven by madness could do?

"You had better have a good story to tell at Henny's when all this is done," Harvey said.

"I'm sure you'll have your own stories to tell."

Harvey grinned. "I guess we'll just have to see who can tell the bigger lies when we get down to remembering."

He and Bennett pushed the rowboat into deeper water and began paddling against the current to get back into the downtown area.

Jake walked to Oldtown Road. The area didn't have the best reputation in Cumberland. Jake had certainly been called out here for more than his fair share of incidents. He'd been here for speakeasy raids, drunk and disorderly calls, fights, car accidents and even a murder. It wasn't too far from Wineow Street, which was underwater at the moment.

Wineow Street had been quiet tonight. The bars and clubs that weren't flooded out had been closed. Jake and the McIntyres had passed dark window after dark window and saw no one inside the bars.

It reminded him of the days of Prohibition when the businesses had appeared closed, but were actually selling black-market booze in windowless rooms.

Jake climbed the hill until he came to the intersection of Maryland and Virginia Avenues. He turned right for no other reason than that was the direction where most of the businesses were. He stopped at the first bar that he found open. The awning said the place was Tam's.

Jake stepped inside the bar.

"Stand in the bucket until you stop dripping," said the bartender.

"If I do that, I'll probably be standing here until Friday," Jake said as he stepped into the barrel.

"Look, buddy, I've been lucky enough to keep the flood out so far. I don't need you or anyone else bringing it in."

"Then come over here and talk to me, or I'm about to track water all over your floor to come over there," Jake said.

The dark-haired bartender frowned. He finished pouring a drink for one man and then came around the end of the bar.

"You had better watch your mouth or I'll toss you out. Then let's see you find a drink," the bartender threatened.

Jake opened up his raincoat so that the bartender could see his navy blue police uniform. The bartender closed his eyes and groaned.

"What do you want?"

"I'm looking for Ray Twigg."

"I don't know him," the bartender said quickly.

"I know he came this way looking for a drink, and as you pointed out, you are the only place open around here. Ray is tall and thin. He has brown hair and a head that looks lopsided."

The bartender nodded. "Yeah. Yeah. I saw him. He came in a bit ago."

"Did he leave?"

"You don't see him here, do you?"

"Don't get smart. He's not in a back room?"

"No, he bought a bottle of Kessler's Private Blend and left. Judging by how he looked, I would say he was going to hole up somewhere, get drunk and try to forget this night," Tam said as he walked back behind the bar.

Jake had no doubt that the man was right. He stepped out of the barrel. He came out of Tam's shaking his head. He looked up into the starless night as if expecting the answer to fall from Heaven.

The Rain Man

No such luck.

Where would Ray be heading now? Was he planning to murder someone else? Was he getting drunk somewhere? Where?

Jake thought about heading back to Ray's room. It wasn't too far away. That seemed too sensible and Ray wasn't acting sensibly. He was over-the-edge crazy.

Still, Jake had no better lead and he had to do something. He started walking down Virginia Avenue looking for anything that might indicate that Ray had been this way.

He stopped before he had gotten fifty yards. It just didn't feel right to be going back to the room at the YMCA.

Mark Connelly had been killed in North End, though Ray and he had met in at bar in South End. So why had Ray gone to all the trouble to get Mark into North End? It didn't make sense.

There was no reason for Ray to have gone there, but maybe, the Rain Man had a reason. Jake frowned. Maybe it wasn't Ray who was causing all of the problems. It might just be the Rain Man.

North End would be closer to the source of the flooding. It just felt right that that was where he should go.

Jake turned and headed back into town. He skirted the flooded area and took Virginia Avenue over to Maryland Avenue. As he was walking along Maryland Avenue, he saw a police car on patrol and stepped into the road to get the cop inside to stop. When the car stopped, Jake ran up beside the driver's side window. Officer George Fisher was inside.

"What are you doing on foot?" George asked him.

"I didn't have much choice. My car's under water on Baltimore Street. Can you give me a ride to my sister's? I've got to talk to someone there before I go out," Jake asked.

George nodded. "Get in."

As they drove down Maryland Avenue, Jake asked, "What do you hear? I haven't been near a radio or headquarters in awhile."

"I heard that the bridges were washed out, but I haven't seen any that were gone yet. Most of them are underwater, though. Now the Western Maryland Railroad Bridge was sagging pretty badly where it crosses Wills Creek. That may have collapsed by now. WTBO is still on the air. I just came down from visiting their station to see what is happening around the area," George told him.

"How'd they manage to stay on the air this late?"

"Senator Tydings got the okay to extend their broadcast because of the emergency. People need to know what's going on, particularly with the phones out."

Jake nodded. "Has anywhere else been hit?"

"I hear that Pennsylvania is bad in the Bedford County area. Around here, Locust Grove started it all. I doubt that there'll be much left there when the water is gone." Jake wondered briefly if the sandbag wall that the folks in Locust Grove had been working on had held. "From George's Creek to Westernport is underwater, too. I'd guess everyone else further down the Potomac is going to be drenched before all this is done, too. Any hotel that still has dry rooms is doing a good business tonight. I checked on a few of them while I was out, and they are filling up quick. And that's the good news."

Jake's eyes widened. "After all that, what could be the bad news?"

"Mayor Legge called in the National Guard to help protect the people of Cumberland and prevent looting. We are basically under martial law now."

Jake was silent for a few moments as he tried to decide whether having the National Guard out was a good thing or a bad one.

"Now that the rain has stopped, how long do you think it will take for the flood waters to go down?" George asked, breaking the silence.

"Does that count emptying it out of people's basements?"

George shrugged. "When those waters go down, they'll be taking half the city with them. I've seen all kinds of things in the water. Stoves, refrigerators, even a piano. This water is tearing through everything. It's knocked down a couple of houses, too."

Jake nodded silently.

George stopped in front of Jake's sister's house.

"This is it, isn't it?" George asked.

"It is. Thanks for the ride. I'll buy you a coffee later this week to thank you," Jake said as he climbed out of the car.

Jake ran up on the porch and knocked on his sister's front door. Virginia answered it.

"Don't just stand outside, Jake. Get in here," she said, waving him inside.

Jake shook his head. "I can't stay, but I need to talk to Chris. Is she all right?"

Virginia nodded, studying her brother. "She's just finishing some soup. What's wrong, Jake?"

"Could you get her, please? I don't want to dawdle more than I have to right now."

Virginia walked away quickly and came back with Chris. She was wearing one of Virginia's robes and slippers. Her red hair was dry but a bit disheveled.

"What's wrong, Jake?" she asked.

"Raymond survived the fall, Chris, and he's moving about the city again. I don't know if he'll try to find you but stay inside."

Jake saw her tense up. "He can't know I'm here."

Jake nodded. "He couldn't have survived that fall either. I don't know what to expect from him so I'm not going to take a chance, especially where you're concerned. Raymond came after you once already. He may do it again."

"What are you going to do?"

"I'm going to find him." He leaned over and kissed Chris. She didn't resist him. "I want you safe."

"I want you safe, too, so don't do anything foolish," Chris replied.

Jake stepped back and hurried back to the road. He was in North End. Hopefully, Ray was, too.

30

Wednesday, March 18, 1936
4:45 a.m.

Raymond staggered as he walked along the railroad tracks. He could see the flood waters rushing down the streets and into the city. The waters filled Cumberland as if the city was in a pot being held under a running faucet.

The faucet had been turned off, though. The rain had stopped. So why did his head still hurt? It throbbed, which is what caused him to stagger. He clutched his head more from instinct than thinking it would help him.

The power of all the Kessler's whiskey he had drunk while walking was wearing off, at least to the point where he could feel the pain in his head again. Yet, he was still drunk and had trouble standing. If only he could have kept his pills. Then he could have ended his pain without drunkenness.

Raymond screamed.

The Rain Man laughed.

Raymond caught sight of a bar on North Centre Street. He left the railroad tracks and sloshed through the water. The flood had reached here and the water was past Raymond's waist, but Raymond's craving for an end to the pain was stronger than his fear of the water.

It was hard to move sideways through the flood current, but he kept his eye on his goal. He was forced to pause after each step and brace himself against the current so he wouldn't be sent floating downstream past the Centre Street Bar and Grill. It took longer to reach than he thought it would, and the pain in his head grew worse all the time.

He reached the entryway and pulled himself out of the current so that the building shielded him from the strongest pull of the current.

Raymond turned the doorknob and discovered that it was locked.

"No!" he screamed.

He pressed his head against the door and stared longingly through the window into the bar. He could see the bar and stools in the shadows. He even caught brief reflections of light off the bottles behind the bar. They would be his salvation if he could only reach them. He could wait out the flood in the bar and feel no pain.

He could leave once the flood waters fell because then the pain would leave with the water. He just needed something to get him through the pain.

He couldn't stop this close to relief.

Raymond punched his fist through the window in the door, ignoring the shards of glass that embedded themselves into his knuckles. He reached through the opening and felt the glass that was still in the frame poke him in the arm.

He groped around for the lock latch on the inside of the door. He found it and turned the lock back. Then he turned the doorknob and opened the door.

It slammed inward as the flood waters rushed inward. The fast-moving current pushed Raymond into the barroom. He wasn't able to disengage his arm from the window quickly enough, and his own weight drove the glass shards into his arm.

Raymond grunted, but he was surprised that the pain didn't hurt as much as his head hurt. The glass in the window frame broke off in his arm and Raymond rolled into the bar, floundering in the waves until he smashed against the bar. He grabbed onto the foot rail to steady himself and get his feet under him.

Raymond stood up and pulled himself around behind the bar. He grabbed the first bottle he found without even looking at what it was. He opened it and drank deeply. The warmth of the alcohol spread throughout his body and Raymond sighed.

He set a few more bottles on the bar. Then he moved around the bar. He picked up a stool and sat down on it. The water nearly reached over the top of the stool.

He took another drink and wondered how long it would be before he stopped feeling the pain in his head. It shouldn't take too long since he had drunk so much on the way from Tam's.

Raymond rolled his arm over and looked at the places where the glass had cut him. He began to carefully pick out the pieces of glass he could see. He should have no trouble washing out the wounds with all the water around him. He could even disinfect it by pouring some of his…he looked at the label on the bottle…rye, Mayflower Rye, on the wound. He also needed to bind it up to stop the bleeding. He probably needed stitches, too. He would have to go to Allegany Hospital. Otherwise, he would have to chance Dr. Evans seeing him.

He took another drink. The pain in his head was beginning to fade. The rye was beginning to work.

He picked a few more shards of glass from his arm. Then he poured the rye into the wounds. It was like pouring fire on his arm. The pain seared through even the peace the alcohol had brought to his head.

Raymond screamed and plunged his arm into the water and shook it. It helped ease the pain somewhat, but he could still feel his arm throbbing. That was the last time he would try that.

"Ray!"

Raymond looked out through the front window. He could see Jake Fairgrieve leaving the railroad tracks, following much the same path that Ray had followed earlier to reach the bar.

No! How had Jake found him? No one knew where he was going, not even Jake! Would he have no rest from the man?

Let me give you the rest you seek, the Rain Man said.

"Yes," Raymond whispered. He could control the pain until it was safe to leave, but he had to do something about Jake Fairgrieve or he would never know peace.

Then let him get closer and I will end it for you.

Raymond took a swig from his bottle and then walked to the open door still holding the bottle in his hand. Jake saw him and hurried his pace.

"Ray!"

As Jake got closer, Raymond felt the power of the Rain Man flow through him. The pain in his arm ceased. He felt so light that he thought that he might float away right out of the water.

The Rain Man was taking control. Then Raymond saw Jake draw his pistol and Raymond was slammed back into his body as the Rain Man fled. Raymond was in total control of his body.

"Put your hands up!" Jake ordered him.

Raymond stared at the pistol. He remembered long ago staring at men when he had been the one holding the pistol or rifle. He remembered also what those weapons could do. He touched his fingers lightly to the side of his skull where he could feel the tough scar tissue.

"Put your hands up, Ray," Jake said again.

Raymond turned and ran back into the bar. He couldn't move fast because of the water, and he kept expecting to feel a bullet hit him in the back.

No shot came, and Raymond ran. At the back end of the bar, there was a short hallway with four doors. He tried each of them. Two led to bathrooms. One led to a staircase, but the fourth was the back door to the bar.

Raymond ran through the door and back into the swiftly moving current. He let himself be carried away by the current, knowing it would move him faster than if he continued to run.

He would escape until the Rain Man could show him how to deal with Jake. Then Jake could be the pursued.

31

Wednesday, March 18, 1936
5:29 a.m.

Jake saw Ray run inside the bar and tried to decide if he should take the shot. He wanted Ray alive to question him about the Rain Man and see what was wrong inside Ray's head.

"Damn!" he muttered to himself as he holstered his pistol.

At least he was sure that Ray wouldn't be taking shots at him. All of Ray's attacks had been physical attacks done hand to hand. That would be reassuring until Jake caught up with Ray.

Jake pushed his way through the current toward the bar. As he began to cross the street, he saw a shadow in the alley. Ray had gone out the back door.

Jake veered into the alley and began to chase Ray in slow-motion pursuit. He had been searching North End for Raymond for hours. Now that Jake had found him, he wasn't going to let Raymond out of his sight. The water swirled around his waist and began to creep up his body as he crossed Mechanic Street. The depth of the water slowed the chase even more and made Jake's footing on the road tenuous, particularly since the current kept pushing sideways against him.

Ray turned south on Mechanic Street and allowed the current to push him along. He kept trying to walk with the current. Jake began to float with the current and gain ground on Ray.

Ray looked over his shoulder and saw Jake coming. He veered onto the Valley Street Bridge. The bridge was water covered but not to the depth of the street. It had been deeper, but the flood waters had been slowly receding through early morning. Ray was able to manage a fast walk through the water.

Jake got his feet under him and ran after Ray. He was close enough that he dove forward and tackled Ray from behind. The two of them fell forward and splashed into the water.

Water crashed against the side of the bridge sending a heavy spray onto the bridge, filling Jake's mouth with water. Jake raised up on his knees sputtering.

Then Ray hit him in the mouth. Jake tumbled backwards and Ray was on top of him. Ray grabbed Jake by the ears and began to squeeze hard as if he wanted to crush Jake's skull.

Jake threw his arms up between Ray's arms to break his hold. As Ray momentarily lost his balance, Jake pushed Ray off of him.

Another wave of water came over the edge of the bridge. Jake heard a few foolhardy spectators who were on the bridge yell in surprise as the cold water hit them.

"Lord, there's a gas tank floating in the river," one man yelled.

"It'll explode if it hits us," a second person said.

Jake looked north and saw one of the tanks from the American Oil Company near the Narrows roll into the river. The oval logo on the tank appeared and then rolled underwater.

Pain flared through his back as Ray smashed a chair that had washed onto the bridge across Jake's back. Jake fell forward and his face went under the shallow water on the bridge.

He felt Ray on his back. Ray lifted Jake's head and tried to smash it against the road bed on the bridge. However, the water on the bridge cushioned Jake's head and kept him from being seriously hurt.

A huge surge of water hit on the side of the bridge and Jake thought he could actually feel the bridge shake under the impact.

The water splashed up and over the bridge. Hundreds of gallons of water smashed down on Ray and Jake. Jake felt himself rolling to the side as the water even obscured Ray from his sight. He slid along the surface of the bridge as the water spread quickly. He felt something hard hit him in the side and thought it must be the side of the bridge.

And then he was falling.

Jake hit the water head first and sank quickly. Then he felt himself rising, and he kicked to help himself surface. Of course, he didn't know how he was going to stay afloat once he got to the surface. He didn't know how to swim!

His head broke the water and he gulped in the air and a good amount of water, too.

Something hit him in the jaw and his head snapped back. He turned and saw Ray at his side.

Jake swung his arms back and forth wildly. He should be able to stay afloat. It couldn't be hard to swim. Just about any kid knew how to swim. He should at least be able to keep from drowning.

Ray hit him again. This time in the ear.

Jake had seen the punch coming, but he was so busy trying to stay afloat that he didn't have time to raise his arm to block the punch.

If Jake was going to stay afloat, he was going to need something to stay afloat on. There was plenty of debris in the water, but Jake was unsure of how some of it was staying afloat. There were metal pipes, cans, and tires as well as trees, brush and wooden items.

Ray hit him again.

Suddenly Jake realized what he could use to stay afloat. He threw himself at Ray and grabbed him around the chest. Ray's attention suddenly shifted from hitting Jake to staying afloat himself.

They spun around and around in the water. Ray dove underwater, but Jake held on because he Ray would come up at some point. When Ray finally surfaced, Jake felt a sense of success. If he could just hold on until they could get to a bank, Jake would be able to arrest Ray.

Then Jake saw the Market Street Bridge rushing to meet them. Ray suddenly swung around as the current slammed both of them up against the center support of the bridge.

Jake yelled in pain and let go of Ray. He started to slide under the water until he reached up and grabbed hold of an edge of the concrete piling. The water kept pounding against him and a barrel nearly missed hitting him. It passed to the side and went under the bridge, which was nearly underwater itself.

Ray grabbed hold of Jake's head and slammed it against the concrete. Pain flared through Jake's head. He tried to fight back but he only had one free hand to fend off Ray because he had to keep himself afloat by holding onto the piling with his other hand.

Behind Ray, Jake saw the large gasoline tank roll under the Valley Street Bridge and head toward them. The tank must not have been full in order to float, but it was still heavy and heading right for them. It was so large that it would almost certainly hit them.

Jake backhanded Ray and tried to push him underwater. Ray let himself drop lower than Jake could reach and he surfaced again in front of Jake. He glanced once again at the gasoline tank as it rolled and swirled toward him. Then he made a decision.

He let go of the concrete piling and rolled to the side so that he could slide under the bridge. As he did, he began to sink into the water.

What a choice, he thought. *Get smashed or drown.*

32

Wednesday, March 18, 1936
6:08 a.m.

Raymond saw Jake slip below the water and smiled because it was obvious from the way that Jake had been clutching at him that Jake couldn't swim. In the end, even Jake had to succumb to the power of the Rain Man. The Rain Man had won as he always did.

There will be no stopping me, the Rain Man said.

Raymond held his arms in the air while he treaded water and cheered loudly.

The Rain Man was right. With Jake gone, there would be no one who could harm him. He would be free!

But first he had to get out of Wills Creek.

Raymond turned and saw the gasoline tank bearing down on him as it rolled and spun in the current. It was only a few yards away.

"No!"

He swam to the side to try and get out of the way, but the tank was too wide. He moved to swim under the bridge, but he was too late.

The tank slammed into him, crushing him against the center bridge support. The tank pinned Raymond, folding itself around him and the bridge, so that he couldn't move. All Raymond could see was darkness and shadows moving.

Yet, for the first time in years, there was no pain. His head did not feel as if it was being squeezed flat.

Raymond smiled and sighed. Such a beautiful feeling to be completely free from the pain and completely free from the Rain Man.

Then he slid slowly under the water and the Rain Man swallowed Raymond.

33

Wednesday, March 18, 1936
3:05 p.m.

Jake woke up with the sun shining in the window. He was surprised to see the sun. After two days of rain, he had come to believe that there was no sun in the world, only water.

He stared at it for awhile, squinting into the bright light and feeling the warmth on his face.

"You're going to blind yourself."

Jake rolled his head to the side and saw Chris sitting in a rocking chair next to the bed.

Bed?

The last thing he remembered was letting himself go under the water to get away from the gasoline tank. He had figured that he would drown. He tried to remember if he had been able to surface again, but for the life of him, he couldn't remember.

"Where are we?" Jake asked.

"Your sister's house," Chris told him.

"I'm surprised Virginia's not in here fussing over me."

"She wanted to be, but we drew cards. I got the high card," Chris said, smiling.

Jake chuckled and it turned into a cough. Chris put her hand on his forehead checking for his temperature. Jake enjoyed the touch of her soft hand against his skin.

"You've got a mild fever and have been battered pretty badly, but you'll be all right. I had to stitch up your head a bit. You had a couple deep cuts. Your skull was too hard to break, though," Chris said.

"Are you here as my doctor or my girlfriend?" Jake asked.

"Does it matter if your girlfriend is a doctor?" Chris countered.

"How did I get here? I don't remember."

"The creek spit you out."

"What?"

The Rain Man

"When the water sprayed up over the Baltimore Street Bridge, it left you behind. Harvey McIntyre was there helping people get across the bridge. He recognized you and brought you here. He said he was a friend of yours," Chris told him.

Jake nodded and looked back outside. The sun felt great. He was surprised at how much he had missed it.

"What about Raymond?" he asked, almost dreading the answer.

"Is that why you were in the water?"

Jake nodded. "He survived the fall from the bank building."

"So you told me," Chris said.

"I found him after I left here last night. We were fighting and got knocked into the creek. I saw a gasoline tank floating in the water and coming toward us so I went underwater," Jake explained.

"Well, he didn't survive the river. The tank hit him," Chris said.

"Are you sure?"

"His body was found mixed in with a pile of debris under the Western Maryland Railroad Bridge near where the Potomac and Wills Creek meet. He was dead. I signed the death certificate."

Jake wondered how many other people had died during the flood. He only thought about it for a moment because this was no time to dwell on death. He was alive. That was something to celebrate.

"Can you swim?" Jake asked.

Chris nodded. "Sure. I haven't for a few years, but I know how."

"Can you teach me?"

"Maybe we can start while we're camping."

Jake smiled as Chris kissed him.

HISTORICAL AFTERWORD

Our Legacy of Floods Part 2

By Albert L. Feldstein

The pursuit and subsequent death of Raymond Twigg, the Rain Man, concluded a series of particularly brutal Cumberland murders. Unfortunately, it would not be long after the waters receded from the great St. Patrick's Day Flood of March 17, 1936, that the City of Cumberland would again be deluged and continue along with its watery destiny.

Heavy rainfall was the major contributing factor for the flood of April 26, 1937. Although well below the recorded Cumberland flood-gauge heights of 1889, 1924, and 1936, this 1937 flood did exceed the 1924 flood level along many other portions of the Potomac River. The flood not only damaged roads and washed out bridges along the basin, but also succeeded in flooding portions of the downtown Cumberland area.

It would be the flood of October 15, 1942, which produced one of the last really significant deluges within the City of Cumberland. At 5 p.m. on the 15th, the flood waters crested on the North Branch of the Potomac River near the city. Although the crest was several feet below the floods of June 1889 and March 1936, it was high enough to flood downtown to a depth of four to five feet. All business was suspended and the Maryland State Guard was called in to restore order. Over 300 people required Red Cross assistance in the form of shelter and canteen service, and over 600 telephones were out of service due to cable and line damage. The cellars of many homes along Wills Creek, which was out of its banks for ten hours, were flooded, as was the basement of City Hall. The local chamber of commerce estimated property damage exceeding $50,000.

The Rain Man

As indicated earlier in the foreword, a flood-protection project for Cumberland was initially conceived when the flood of 1924, and the later flood of 1936 inflicted severe damage to the city. By 1945, the Army Corps of Engineers had begun to restudy their earlier flood-control construction designs, and during the post-war period, steps were undertaken to plan for the construction of the flood-control project. By March 1949, the work was underway. The Cumberland, Maryland-Ridgeley, West Virginia Flood Control Project was completed in May 1959. The total cost was $18,500,000. The federal government provided $15,600,000, and the local community provided $2,900,000. The City of Cumberland paid Ridgeley, West Virginia's share. One highway and one railroad bridge were removed. Three highway and two railway bridges were reconstructed, and three pumping stations (which were to prove invaluable during the floods of 1996) with a combined capacity of 166,000 gallons per minute were constructed to remove storm drainage from behind the levees and walls during times of flood. A total of fifty Cumberland and seventy Ridgeley buildings were either razed or relocated.

A major problem of planning and design was the provision of facilities to pass a major flood through Wills Creek where urban development had encroached on the flood plain. As finally constructed, the concrete channel in Wills Creek will pass a flow of 50,000 cubic feet of water per second, or 131 percent of the maximum flow recorded in March 1936. On the North Branch, upstream from the mouth of Wills Creek, levees and flood walls on both banks were constructed to confine a flow of 93,000 cubic feet per second. Downstream from the mouth of Wills Creek, the North Branch channel was straightened, widened and deepened and levees and slope protection constructed. This channel was built to safely pass a flood volume of 113,000 cubic feet of water per second, or 128 percent of the maximum flow recorded in 1936.

These channel improvements can be seen today from the bridge crossing the North Branch into Ridgeley, West Virginia, from Greene Street at the mouth of Wills Creek. When the project was completed in 1959, over forty years ago, it was estimated at that time a recurrence of the 1936 flood would cause in excess of eight million dollars in damage in the City of Cumberland if the project did not exist.

Among those who helped lay the groundwork for the construction of the Cumberland Maryland-Ridgeley, West Virginia Flood Control

Construction Project and see it through to its eventual completion were Mayors George W. Legge and Thomas Koon of Cumberland, who along with Congressman David J. Lewis and the U.S. Senators from Maryland and West Virginia, helped push for early federal action to authorize funds for flood-control protection under the administration of Franklin Delano Roosevelt. The actual construction occurred during the terms of office of Mayors Thomas S. Post, 1944-1952; Roy W. Eves, 1952-1958 and J. Edwin Keech, 1958-1962. The Army Corps of Engineers had been involved from the beginning, since at least the 1924 flood, in assisting the City of Cumberland with its flood protection. It was during the administration of Mayor Roy W. Eves, with C. Z. Nuzum as the city engineer, that four bridges were constructed over Wills Creek and the Potomac River. These were the Valley Street Bridge in 1954-1955, the Market Street Bridge in 1956, the Baltimore Street Bridge in 1957-1958 and the Blue Bridge (over the Potomac River) in 1955. J. Glenn Beall, Sr. served in the U.S. House of Representatives from 1943 to 1953 and the U.S. Senate from 1953 to 1965. This encompassed the flood-control construction years. Along with other federal representatives, he continued to help secure construction funds and also worked to fund other flood-control protection measures along the Potomac River, such as the Savage River Dam in Garrett County which went into operation in 1952. The two primary contractors/construction companies for the project were E.G. Albrecht of Chicago and the George F. Hazelwood Company in Cumberland.

There have been other significant deluges in this area not covered in the historical foreword. During the construction of the flood project, downtown Cumberland and Wills Creek experienced some flooding in 1957 that actually washed away some of the flood-control construction equipment. Hurricane Agnes in 1972 caused a lot of damage along the C&O Canal and Potomac River. Hyndman, Pennsylvania, has experienced terrible damage in recent years, and the flood of 1985 was devastating, particularly along the South Branch of the Potomac River Valley where the loss of life, as well as property occurred. A few days after the January 1996 flood, I had lunch with a friend of mine who had "had" a camp down at Millenson's on the South Branch. He told me that, at least at his spot on the river, the water mark from 1985 was eight feet higher than in 1996.

This brings us to the present. In just a sixteen-month period, beginning in June 1995 and again in January and September of 1996, the

The Rain Man

Western Maryland region was severely impacted by a series of devastating deluges, with each of these three flooding events being classified as a 100-year flood. The January 1996 event was the result of a rapid snowmelt from a blizzard occurring earlier in the month. The flooding in September 1996 was a consequence of the heavy rainfall from Tropical Storm Fran. Both of these resulted in Presidential Disaster Declarations.

These flooding events led to the appointment of a "Western Maryland Flood Task Force" comprised of representatives from the four Western Maryland counties of Garrett, Allegany, Washington and Frederick. As of this writing, it remains the mission and continuing responsibility of this task force to recommend and implement measures that can be taken to reduce the risk to life and property from future flooding within the region. Since these flooding events, the task force has helped to secure over sixty million dollars in funding for an array of flood mitigation, restoration and infrastructure repair projects and studies. This included the acquisition and razing of twenty-seven homes located along Front Street in Westernport which were heavily damaged during the floods. The site is now the home of Creekside Park.

Our vulnerability, that continuing historical relationship we have with the forces of nature, again became evident in September 2000 when a sudden and swift storm dropped up to six inches of rain. With most of the damage centered upon Cumberland's west side, thirty-two structures reported major damage, 141 suffered minor damage and three were destroyed. Numerous homes and several businesses were impacted, and several cars were washed away. In the words of one veteran local observer, "In my thirty-five years with the National Weather Service, I've never seen places flooded that were flooded here tonight." Most recently, in June 2001, heavy rains and the resulting run-off again caused significant property damage. This time the areas impacted were along Route 220, as well as Westernport.

Thank you, and always remember to keep your head above water.

December 28, 2001

About the Author

James is the author of four other novels, including the historical novel *Canawlers*. He is also a reporter with the *Cumberland Times-News* in Cumberland, Maryland. His interest in the 1936 St. Patrick's Day Flood developed from an article he did about the flood on its sixty-fifth anniversary.

He lives with his wife, Amy, and son, Ben, in Cumberland and is currently at work on his next novel.

If you would like to be kept up to date on new books being published by James or ask him questions, he can be reached by e-mail at jimrada@yahoo.com.